DRAKORIA

A JOURNEY BEYOND WORLDS

NISHI SHAH

Dedicated to my mom and dad,

Amisha Shah and Ritesh Shah

"Your love will always be imprinted on the heart of mine"

To all readers of **"DRAKORIA"** who pick up this book,

thank you for giving my words a chance:)

Contents

THIS BOOK BELONGS TO:

____

Thank you! for Exploring "DRAKORIA"...

Acknowledgements

Them that I love, Know that I love them. Special thanks to my dear readers who made this journey worthwhile.Writing a book is harder than i thought and more rewarding than i could have ever imagined. it takes a large ground of readers to help even a small book blast off.

The helping hands of this books includes my mom and dad, I owe you a huge debt of gratitude for supporting me and always beleiving in me. My Grandpa, Pravin Shah and My sister, Jainy Shah, who always supported me and my brother Jinay Shah, who always helped me in things he can.

I would like to thank my teachers Mrs. Swapna Menon, Mrs. Priya Nishant, Mrs. Sheetal Mukherjee , Mr. Siddhart Sharma , Mr Jaimish Patel and my all other teachers and principal Dr. Sanjay mehta of Countryside international school, Surat, Gujarat, India ,who have helped me reach this point and turning my vision into reality.

Also a big thanks to my best preceptors Mr.Rony modi , Mr. Abhi Mehta and Mr.Mitesh Mehta for teaching me self-discipline, true life values, ethical values and moral values and help me shape my personality as a better human being.

And finally a special thanks to my partners , best of my friends, Heny , Mishthi , Helli, Krupam ,Veer, Mahir, Jash, Vraj, Pearly, Yashasvi, Rahi and evryone who helped me by sharing there ideas and didn't let me stop and kept me on my way. And also if you are able to made it till end... Impressive!

Foreword

There are stories told in whispers, hidden in the folds of time, waiting for the right souls to uncover them. This is one of those stories. Its origins are lost to the ages, its truths cloaked in shadows, and its path known only to those who dare follow it."

"Victor, Clara, Brumble, and Gruffle are not ordinary travelers. They have been called by forces beyond their understanding, drawn into a struggle against an ancient darkness that threatens to unravel their world. Their quest is not simply one of power or glory—it is a journey that will test their very souls."

"But they are not alone. An ancient dragon, Milo-Blaze, has watched over the secrets of the world for centuries, guiding them toward the Holy Drake Book—a key to trapping Noxmire's dark spirit. Yet, even the book's power is shrouded in mystery, its true nature known to few. What lies within its pages is as much a puzzle as a weapon, and its consequences may be more than any of them can bear."

"So, as you turn the pages of this tale, know this: What you read may change you. The questions it raises may stay with you long after the last word. For this story is not just about saving a world—it is about discovering what lies beyond the veil of the unknown.

Preface

"In a world where the threads of fate intertwine with the power of dragons, there are those who rise in defiance of darkness, and those who fall prey to it. This is the story of four unlikely companions—Victor, Clara, Brumble, and Gruffle—each driven by their own desires, fears, and dreams. Their paths cross when an ancient and malevolent force, Noxmire, stirs from its long slumber, threatening to unravel the very fabric of their world."

"Guided by the mysterious dragon Milo-Blaze, whose wisdom spans eons, they embark on a journey fraught with peril and sacrifice. To defeat Noxmire, they must retrieve the Holy Drake Book, an artifact of unimaginable power, and unlock its secrets. But the journey is not simply about strength—it is about choosing the right path when faced with impossible choices, testing their bonds and resolve with each step."

"This is not just a tale of magic and monsters. It is a tale of friendship, courage, and the battle to keep hope alive when the shadows of the world seem all-encompassing. In the end, it is not the power they wield that will determine their victory, but the heart and will that guides them to their fate."

1

"Victor Halloway always believed there were places the world wasn't meant to see. But when the whispers began—the ones only he could hear—he realized those places might already be watching him."

Victor Halloway was a man who made the impossible seem easy. At just 28 years old, he had already built a life most people could only dream of. He wasn't just an entrepreneur—he was a genius, the kind of person who could see connections where no one else could. People admired him, but more than that, they were in awe of him.

Victor's life seemed perfect. He was happily married to Clara, the love of his life. Clara wasn't just his wife; she was a brilliant archaeologist with a sharp mind and a fearless heart. Together, they were unstoppable—a team that blended Victor's endless curiosity with Clara's love for uncovering ancient mysteries.

But Victor wasn't like other people. Even as a child, he had always been fascinated by the unknown. While other kids played games, Victor was busy taking apart his father's expensive watches. He would carefully disassemble them, studying every little gear and spring, and then put them back together again so perfectly that his father never even noticed.

His teachers said he was gifted, but Victor didn't just want to learn what the world already knew—he wanted to discover what no one else had ever imagined. He excelled in everything he studied, but his true love was theoretical physics, where the lines between science and magic sometimes seemed to blur.

Yet there was always something more to Victor, something no one could quite understand. His fascination with fantasies wasn't just a childhood phase—it was a spark deep inside him, a hunger to know what lay beyond the veil of ordinary life. And while Victor's world seemed perfect, there was a strange shadow over it, like a whisper only he could hear, calling him toward something greater... and far more dangerous.

Victor Halloway lived in a huge mansion that everyone thought was perfect. But no one knew its biggest secret. Deep beneath the floors of the mansion, hidden behind a door only Victor and Clara could find, was a secret lab. This wasn't just any lab—it was a strange, quiet place where the air felt heavy, and shadows seemed to move when no one was looking.

Victor spent long nights in this lab, working on things he never told anyone about. He said he was searching for something big—something so important it could change the world. The walls were covered in strange drawings, old maps, and notes written in a language no one could understand. Strange machines hummed softly in the corners, and glowing lights flickered like stars in the dark. Sometimes, Clara would sit with him, watching him work, though even she didn't always know what he was looking for.

Victor and Clara loved to explore strange and spooky places. On holidays, they didn't go to beaches or sunny parks. Instead, they went to old, crumbling castles where the wind howled through the empty halls. They climbed into deep, dark caves that seemed to whisper secrets from the shadows. They wandered through ancient ruins, where the stones were cold, and the air felt like it was holding its breath.

Victor didn't just love these places because they were beautiful. He felt like they were calling to him. He believed they held clues to something bigger—something hidden. Clara always went with him, her heart brave and curious. She said she wasn't afraid of ghosts or shadows, but sometimes, even she felt like they were being watched.

Even when they were far away on their adventures, Victor's mind was always on his lab. He believed everything they found was part of a puzzle—pieces of a secret so big that most people couldn't even imagine it.

But lately, Victor had been acting strange. He spent more time in the lab, and sometimes Clara heard him talking to himself late at night. She asked him if he was okay, but Victor only smiled and said, "I'm so close, Clara. So close."

Neither of them knew that their next trip would be different. This time, they wouldn't just find old ruins or strange caves. This time, something would find them.

Clara often wondered what Victor was doing in his secret lab. She wasn't allowed inside, and whenever she asked him about it, he would just smile and change the subject. "You wouldn't understand," he would say with a playful grin, but there was something in his eyes—something that made Clara uneasy.

Sometimes, late at night, she would hear strange noises coming from the lab. It sounded like machines whirring, papers shuffling, and even faint whispers, though she knew Victor was alone. Clara didn't like to admit it, but she was starting to feel afraid. What if something went wrong? What if Victor was working on something dangerous?

Victor, however, was too focused to notice her worries. He was chasing something big—bigger than anything he had ever worked on before. He had picked up a strange signal, one that didn't come from Earth or anything known. It was faint, like a whisper carried on the wind, but it was enough to spark his curiosity.

He traced the signal back to its origins, but there was a problem. He didn't know the exact location. The clues he found were scattered and strange: ancient maps with markings that didn't make sense, symbols written in a language no one could read, and old, crumbling books that seemed older than time itself.

Victor was convinced that all these pieces were connected. The signal, the maps, the language—it all pointed to something hidden, something long forgotten. But what was it? And why did it feel like the signal was calling to him specifically?

Clara watched as Victor worked harder and harder, the light in his lab glowing late into the night. She wanted to trust him, but deep down, she felt a chill she couldn't explain. Whatever Victor had found, it wasn't just a discovery. It was something waiting to be found.

And Clara couldn't shake the feeling that when Victor found it, everything would change—maybe for the worse.

Victor loved compasses more than anything. He had so many of them in his secret lab—big ones, tiny ones, shiny ones, and old rusty ones. Each compass was special to him. He said they had secrets, that they always knew where to go, even when no one else did. His lab shelves were full of them, and sometimes he just sat there, staring at them, wondering where they might lead.

One stormy evening, Victor was working late in his lab. The rain was loud, tapping against the windows, and the wind made strange, whistling sounds. Victor didn't notice. He was too busy studying his maps and the old papers he had found through the mysterious signal. The maps were covered in strange symbols, and the papers were written in an odd language that no one could understand. Victor had been working on this puzzle for weeks, but nothing made sense.

He sighed and ran his hands through his hair. "What am I missing?" he whispered to himself.

Then, suddenly, the lights in his lab flickered and went out, leaving him in the dark. Outside, the rain got heavier, and thunder rumbled in the distance. Victor lit a candle and placed it on his desk. The warm, flickering light filled the room, but the moment it did, something strange happened.

The compasses on the shelves began to shake. At first, they wobbled softly, but then they started spinning wildly. Victor froze, his eyes wide. He had never seen anything like this before. The compasses spun faster and faster, and then, to his shock, they floated into the air.

One by one, the compasses rose and began circling around him. They moved faster and faster, forming a glowing ring of light. Victor couldn't move; he could only watch as the light from the compasses grew brighter and brighter. The air buzzed with energy, and a strange hum filled the room.

The maps on his desk flew into the air, spinning around him like the compasses. Books toppled from the shelves, and papers scattered everywhere. It was like a storm inside his lab. Victor felt dizzy, and the bright light made his eyes hurt. He thought he could hear whispers, but he couldn't tell where they were coming from. It felt like the compasses were alive, like they were trying to tell him something important.

"Stop!" he shouted, but the compasses didn't stop. They spun even faster, and the glowing light grew so bright that it filled the whole room. Victor's head spun, and he couldn't keep his eyes open any longer. Everything went black.

When Victor woke up, everything was quiet. The compasses were back on their shelves, perfectly still. The maps were neatly stacked on his desk, and the books were back in their places, as if nothing had happened.

"Victor, wake up," Clara said softly, shaking his shoulder. "You've been working too long. Come to bed."

Victor sat up, his heart pounding. He looked around the lab, trying to make sense of what had happened. He told Clara about the flying compasses, the bright light, and how it felt like they were trying to tell him something.

Clara smiled and shook her head. "It was just a bad dream," she said. "You're tired, that's all."

But Victor wasn't sure. He knew what he saw. It wasn't a dream. The compasses had moved, the light had shone, and the whispers had been real. Something strange had happened in his lab, and he couldn't shake the feeling that it wasn't over.

Victor sat there, staring at the compasses. Were they trying to guide him somewhere? What were they trying to say? He didn't have the answers, but one thing was certain—this was just the beginning.

Clara could see how tired Victor was. He had been working too hard in his lab, and his face looked tense all the time. She cared about him so much, and it worried her. One evening, she gently placed her hand on his and said, "Victor, if you love me, promise me you won't go to the lab for a few days. Just take a break, please."

Victor looked at her. He could see the worry in her eyes, and it made his heart ache. He loved his work, but he loved Clara even more. He sighed and nodded. "Alright, Clara. No lab for a few days. I promise."

Clara smiled and told him she had a surprise for him—a trip to the Carpathian Mountains. It was a beautiful place, full of forests and ancient caves. Clara knew Victor loved exploring mysterious places, and she thought this would help him relax.

When they reached the Carpathian Mountains, Victor was still thinking about that strange night in his lab. He couldn't stop wondering—was it a dream, or had it been real? But he didn't want to ruin the trip for Clara, so he pushed the thoughts away and focused on her. They spent their days exploring the beautiful city near the mountains, tasting new foods, and enjoying the fresh, crisp air.

On the last day of the trip, they planned to visit the deep caves. Clara was excited, and Victor, though still distracted, was curious too. They joined a small group led by a tour guide and an instructor. The guide told them stories about the caves—how they were ancient, dark, and full of secrets.

As they entered the caves, Victor felt a chill. The air was cold and damp, and the walls seemed to hum softly, like they were alive. The group moved deeper and deeper, their flashlights casting long, eerie shadows on the rocky walls.

At first, Victor tried to enjoy the trip, listening to the guide's stories and holding Clara's hand. But as they went further into the caves, he started to feel something strange. It was a familiar feeling—the same energy he had felt that creepy night in his lab.

The air seemed heavier now, and Victor's heart started to race. The deeper they went, the stronger the feeling became. It was like the cave was pulling him in, whispering to him, calling to him. He tried to ignore it, but it was too strong. He couldn't shake the feeling that something was waiting for him in the darkness.

Victor looked at Clara. She was smiling, fascinated by the stories and the beauty of the caves. He didn't want to scare her, so he stayed quiet. But inside, he was filled with dread. What was this energy? And why did it feel so familiar?

As they walked deeper into the cave, Victor couldn't help but think: maybe the answers he had been searching for weren't in his lab. Maybe they were here, waiting for him in the shadows of the ancient caves.

The deeper they went into the cave, the heavier the air felt. Victor's strange feeling grew stronger with every step. It was as if the walls were closing in, and the whispers in his mind were growing louder. Suddenly, his chest felt tight. He couldn't breathe properly.

Victor stopped walking, his hand gripping his chest. His breathing became loud and fast, echoing through the cave. Clara turned to him, her face full of worry. "Victor! What's wrong?" she asked, her voice trembling.

Everyone in the group stopped and stared. The guide and the instructor exchanged uneasy glances. "It's normal," the instructor said, trying to sound calm. "The air gets thinner down here. It happens sometimes."

"Normal?" Clara snapped, her voice rising. "How is this normal? He's having a panic attack! He can't breathe!" She was furious. "We're leaving. Right now!"

She grabbed Victor's hand and wrapped her arm around him to steady him. Without waiting for anyone's permission, she turned and began dragging him back toward the cave's entrance. Victor stumbled along beside her, his breaths still shallow and fast.

The way back felt endless. Every step was heavy, but as they got closer to the entrance, the strange energy started to fade. By the time they reached the mouth of the cave, Victor could breathe again. The fresh mountain air hit his face, and he took a deep, shaky breath.

Clara held onto him tightly, her eyes filled with worry. "Victor, are you okay? Talk to me! Please!"

Victor nodded, still catching his breath. "I'm fine now," he said softly, his voice weak but steady. "It's over."

Clara didn't look convinced, but she didn't push him. Victor took her hand, squeezing it tightly, as if to reassure her—and himself. He didn't let go of her hand the entire way back to the city.

As they walked in silence, Victor couldn't shake the feeling that the cave hadn't just been a bad experience. It had been something more—something waiting for him, something trying to reach him. But for now, he stayed quiet, focusing on Clara and the warmth of her hand in his.

2

After leaving the caves, Clara and Victor decided to stop at a small café in the heart of the city. The air was crisp, and the streets were alive with chatter and the glow of warm lights. They walked into the cozy café, the smell of fresh coffee and baked goods wrapping around them like a comforting hug.

Victor quickly ordered his favorite—a hot latte. Clara, feeling adventurous, chose something new from the menu: Carpathian Matcha. They sat at a small table by the window, sipping their drinks and talking for hours. Clara laughed at Victor's stories, and Victor felt a little lighter, grateful for this moment of peace.

When they finished their drinks, the night was still young. "Let's explore a bit more," Clara suggested. Victor agreed, and they strolled through the charming streets, admiring the old buildings and vibrant shops.

As they walked, Victor's eyes caught something unusual—a small, dusty store with a wooden sign that read "Antiques and Mysteries." The storefront had an old, almost forgotten charm, with cobwebs clinging to the edges of its windows.

"Let's check it out," Victor said, his curiosity piqued.

Inside, the store felt like stepping into another time. It was dimly lit, with shelves and tables crammed with ancient artifacts, mysterious trinkets, and odd curiosities.

Clara and Victor wandered through the aisles, marveling at the strange items—jars of faded maps, books with cracked leather covers, and tools whose purposes were long forgotten.

Then, Clara's eyes landed on something unusual. "Victor, come look at this!" she called, pointing to a small, dusty corner of the shop.

Victor walked over and froze when he saw it. It was a compass—unlike any he had ever seen. It was old, rusty, and oddly shaped, but it gleamed with strange, glowing colors that seemed to shift in the dim light. The surface was textured, almost alive, with patterns that looked like they were etched by no human hand. It felt... otherworldly.

Victor's heart raced as he picked it up, turning it over in his hands. The compass felt warm, almost like it was alive. He knew, in that moment, he had to have it.

He called for the shop owner, a gray-haired man with tired eyes and a cautious smile. "I want to buy this," Victor said, holding up the compass.

The owner's expression changed to one of surprise. "Are you sure?" he asked, his voice low. "That compass has been here for years. No one even looks at it. And... well, it's not cheap. It's worth millions. People think it's just old junk."

Victor didn't hesitate. "I'm sure," he said firmly. "I collect compasses. It's the only thing I love to collect, and this one... this one is special."

The shop owner stared at him for a moment, then shrugged. "Alright, it's your choice," he said. "But don't say I didn't warn you. This compass... it's strange."

Victor handed over the payment without a second thought, clutching the compass tightly. Clara watched him, a mix of curiosity and concern on her face. "Victor, why this one?" she asked as they stepped out of the shop.

Victor looked at her, then back at the glowing, rusty compass in his hands. "I don't know," he admitted, his voice soft. "But it feels like it's meant for me."

As they walked back to their hotel, Victor couldn't shake the feeling that this compass wasn't just an ordinary artifact. It felt like it had been waiting for him, and now, for better or worse, it was his.

A few days passed, and Victor and Clara were back at their mansion. Life felt normal again, and Clara was glad to see Victor smiling more. One morning, Victor walked up to Clara, grinning. "Ma'am," he said in a playful tone, "may I return to my lab now?"

Clara gave him an unamused look but sighed and said, "Fine. Just don't overwork yourself, okay?"

Victor hugged her tightly. "Nothing's wrong. Stop worrying," he said with a warm smile before heading to his secret lab.

As Victor stepped inside, he felt a strange joy. It felt good to be back, surrounded by his gadgets, maps, and of course, his precious collection of compasses. But now, at the center of it all, stood the old Carpathian compass. He had placed it on a pedestal, making it the main attraction of his lab. Anyone entering would notice it immediately—though no one ever entered except Victor and Clara.

Victor treated the compass with care, dusting it daily and admiring its strange, glowing patterns. Clara noticed how much it meant to him and was glad to see him happy again.

One stormy evening, Victor decided to clean his lab. He was carefully wiping down his equipment when the rain started. At first, it was gentle, but soon it turned into a raging storm. The wind howled outside, and thunder boomed so loudly it shook the windows.

Victor paused, staring out the small window in his lab. The lights flickered once, twice, and then went out completely. He sighed, used to these interruptions, and lit a candle, just as he had done before.

But as soon as the candlelight filled the room, the compass on the pedestal started to move. Slowly at first, then faster. It began to glow—so brightly that it lit up the entire lab.

Victor froze, his breath catching in his throat. All the other compasses in the room began to spin wildly, their needles pointing in every direction. The old Carpathian compass rose into the air, its glow intensifying. It spun faster and faster, creating a bright, swirling light.

Then, it happened.

A portal—black as night but surrounded by blinding, beaming lights—opened in the center of the room. It looked like a rip in space, twisting and turning, pulling everything toward it.

Victor stood still, his eyes wide with both terror and awe. He couldn't move, couldn't think. The room was filled with a strange hum, almost like a song from another world.

And then, in an instant of clarity, everything clicked. The maps, the signals, the strange energy he had felt in the cave—all of it led to this. The compass wasn't just an artifact; it was the key.

Victor's hand trembled as he reached for the candle. With a deep breath, he blew it out.

The lab went dark. The spinning stopped. The compasses fell silent, and the portal vanished as if it had never been there.

Victor stood alone in the quiet, his heart pounding. He was terrified, yes—but also, deep down, he felt something else. Satisfaction. He had found the answer he had been searching for, even if it scared him to his core.

He looked at the Carpathian compass, now sitting still on its pedestal. It was no longer glowing, but Victor knew—its secrets were far from over.

Victor couldn't shake the memory of the portal from his mind. It haunted him every waking moment, calling to him like a whisper from another world. He knew it was dangerous—perhaps even deadly—but the need for answers burned brighter than his fear.

He sat in his lab, staring at the Carpathian compass. Its quiet stillness felt almost mocking, as if it were daring him to take the next step. And Victor had made up his mind. He would go through the portal.

"I have to know," he whispered to himself, his voice trembling.

Victor began his preparations in secret. He gathered tools, packed supplies, and jotted down notes about the strange maps and symbols he had been studying. He knew he couldn't tell Clara. She would never let him go. So, instead, he wrote her a note—a letter explaining everything.

As he wrote, his hand shook. The words came slowly, heavy with emotion:

"Clara,

If you're reading this, it means I've gone where I must. I didn't want to leave without telling you, but I knew you'd try to stop me. Please understand—this is something I have to do. The answers I've been searching for are on the other side. I don't know what I'll find, or if I'll come back, but I promise I'll do everything to return to you.

I love you more than anything. Always remember that.

—Victor"

He placed the note on her favorite chair, where she'd be sure to find it, and took a deep breath. The thought of leaving her behind tore at his heart, but his curiosity was stronger.

Victor waited for the storm. Every night, he sat by the window, watching the sky for signs of rain. Days passed, then a week, and his resolve only grew stronger.

Finally, the night arrived.

The wind began to howl, and the first drops of rain splattered against the glass. Victor's heart raced. He stood in his lab, his bag of supplies slung over his shoulder, staring at the compass on its pedestal. The storm grew fiercer, and the lights flickered, then went out completely.

Victor lit the candle with trembling hands. The moment the flame came to life, the compasses began to spin, faster and faster, just as they had before. The Carpathian compass rose into the air, glowing with an otherworldly light. The hum filled the room again, growing louder as the portal opened before him.

The swirling black and white vortex loomed, pulling at the edges of reality itself. Victor took a step forward, his legs heavy with fear. He paused, glancing back at the door, as if expecting Clara to burst in and stop him. But the house was silent.

"This is it," he whispered to himself.

He took another step closer to the portal. The air around it felt electric, buzzing with energy that made his skin tingle. His mind screamed at him to stop, to turn back—but he couldn't.

Victor stood at the edge of the portal, the glowing light reflecting in his wide eyes. He took one final deep breath and stepped through.

The world around him shifted and twisted, and then, in an instant, Victor Halloway was gone.

The moment Victor opened his eyes, he felt it—everything was different. His body was heavy, as if an invisible force was pulling him down. The air was thick, almost buzzing with energy, and every breath he took felt strange, like he wasn't supposed to be there.

Victor pushed himself up from the ground, his hands sinking slightly into the soft, glowing moss beneath him. His eyes widened as he looked around. The landscape was like nothing he had ever seen—alien, beautiful, and terrifying all at once.

Neon plants bloomed all around him, their luminous petals pulsing softly, casting eerie shadows. The sky above was a fiery black, swirling with ribbons of red and orange that moved like they were alive. Two massive moons hung in the sky, one pale blue and the other a deep crimson, their light casting an otherworldly glow on everything below. Far in the distance, mountains glowed faintly, as if their very rocks were made of light.

Victor's heart raced. Fear gripped him, but curiosity burned just as brightly. He stood, brushing himself off, and froze.

He wasn't wearing his usual clothes. Instead, he was dressed in a sleek black jumpsuit that clung to him like a second skin. A long black coat billowed slightly in the strange, shifting air. On his wrist, a blue fluorescent band glowed faintly, its light pulsing in rhythm with his heartbeat.

"What... what is this?" Victor muttered, his voice barely audible over the hum of the alien world.

Taking a deep breath to steady himself, he began to walk. His boots crunched softly against the glowing moss, and with every step, he felt the weight of this new world pressing down on him.

"This can't be real," he whispered, though deep down, he knew it was.

The silence was deafening. No wind, no animals, no sounds of life—just the hum of the plants and the faint crackling of energy in the air. The stillness made the place feel even more unsettling. Victor's eyes darted around, searching for any sign of movement, any clue about where he was.

He walked for what felt like hours, his heart pounding with every step. He kept telling himself he was alone, that no life existed here, but he couldn't shake the feeling that he was being watched.

Suddenly, he stopped. His foot hovered over the ground, and he froze mid-step. There, in the glowing moss ahead of him, was something that shouldn't be there—footprints.

They were faint, but unmistakable. They led away from where he stood, disappearing into the distance.

Victor's chest tightened. If there were footprints, it meant he wasn't alone. Someone—or something—had been here before him.

His hands clenched into fists, and he glanced back over his shoulder. The portal was gone. There was no way back.

Swallowing hard, he took another step forward, following the footprints into the unknown.

Victor walked slowly, following the footprints on the ground. They led him to a big, dark cave. The cave looked just like the ones he had seen in the Carpathian Mountains, but this one felt strange, as if it was alive.

He stopped at the entrance and looked inside. A cold wind came from the cave, and it made a soft humming sound. Victor's heart was beating fast. He was scared, but his curiosity pushed him to go in.

The air inside the cave was wet and heavy. It was hard to breathe, but Victor kept walking. The walls of the cave glowed faintly, like they had tiny lights hidden inside. The deeper he went, the louder the humming sound became.

The footprints disappeared, but Victor didn't stop. He felt like the cave was pulling him forward. He turned a corner, and then he saw something strange at the end of the cave.

It was a portal, floating in the air. It swirled with bright colors—blue, red, and black—and it made a loud buzzing noise. Victor stared at it, his eyes wide. It looked beautiful but scary at the same time.

"What is this?" he whispered.

Victor wanted to run away, but he couldn't. The portal felt like it was calling him, asking him to come closer. Slowly, he reached out his hand.

As soon as his hand touched the portal, he felt a strong pull. It yanked him forward, and suddenly he was spinning. Lights flashed all around him, and he heard strange whispers. His body felt heavy, then light, and then heavy again.

THUD!

Victor landed hard on the ground. He groaned and sat up, rubbing his head. When he opened his eyes, he froze.

He was in a forest, but it was not like any forest he had ever seen. The trees were huge, and they glowed with blue and green light. Flowers around him shone like tiny stars. The air was filled with strange sounds—low growls, loud screeches, and a soft humming noise that seemed to come from the ground.

Victor stood up, brushing the dust off his clothes. He looked around, feeling confused and scared. He walked through the glowing trees, carefully moving past the strange plants.

After a while, he reached the edge of the forest. What he saw next made him gasp.

It was the Carpathian city—but everything looked different. The buildings were the same shape, but they glowed softly, like they were made of light. The sky was black and fiery, with two huge moons. One moon was blue, and the other was red. Their light made the whole city look strange and magical.

Victor's heart started beating faster. He didn't understand where he was or how this was possible.

Then he saw them.

The streets were not empty. Tall, thin creatures were walking around. Their eyes glowed, and their bodies moved in strange, jerky ways. They didn't look human at all.

Victor crouched down, trying not to be seen. Suddenly, a loud roar shook the air. He looked up and saw a giant dragon flying across the sky. Its wings were so big that they blocked the moons for a moment. The dragon's shadow fell over the city, and Victor felt a chill run down his spine.

His hands were shaking as he pressed himself against a wall. His mind was spinning. He didn't know where he was or how to get back home.

"What is this place?" he whispered, his voice trembling.

Victor didn't know what to do. All he knew was that he had to be very careful, or he might not survive in this strange, glowing world.

3

Victor pulled up the hood of his coat, trying to blend in with the strange, glowing world around him. His heart raced as he walked through the streets, careful not to draw attention. Everyone around him looked like cartoon monsters—odd shapes, glowing eyes, and limbs that didn't move like humans. Their voices were low growls or eerie whispers.

He moved quickly but quietly, avoiding their stares. As he turned a corner, his eyes fell on something familiar—the ancient compass shop. The same shop he and Clara had visited in the real Carpathian city.

Victor hesitated for a moment, then stepped inside. The shop was dimly lit and eerily silent. Dust floated in the air, and the shelves were covered with strange, glowing trinkets. But there was no shopkeeper, no sign of life.

He walked further inside, his footsteps echoing on the wooden floor. That's when he noticed a strange, creepy door at the back of the shop. It was old and cracked, with a rusty plaque nailed to it. The plaque had something carved on it:

"Eyes on eyes, foots on foots, and there where you keep your blood boots."

Victor frowned, reading the words again and again. It made no sense. He tried to open the door, but as soon as his fingers touched the handle, a sharp spark of energy shot through him. He yelped and stepped back, shaking his hand. The door didn't budge.

He tried again, pushing and pulling with all his strength, but the same spark zapped him every time. Frustrated, he stared at the words on the plaque.

"Eyes on eyes, foots on foots, and there where you keep your blood boots."

"What does that even mean?" Victor muttered to himself.

He looked around the shop for anything that could be a clue. His eyes landed on an odd statue beside the door. It was strange and creepy—a single, huge eye resting on top of a big foot.

Victor's eyes widened. "Eyes on eyes... foots on foots," he whispered. The words clicked in his mind.

He bent down and carefully removed his boots. His heart pounded as he placed them at the base of the statue. The boots fit perfectly into the grooves carved into the foot.

The moment his boots were in place, the statue's giant eye began to glow, and the door creaked. Slowly, it swung open, revealing a dark passage.

A strong wind rushed out of the doorway, almost knocking Victor backward. The wind carried an eerie howl, like a warning, but Victor didn't back away.

He took a deep breath, his hands trembling, and stepped closer to the open door.

"What's behind this?" he whispered, his voice barely audible.

The air grew colder, and Victor could feel his heart pounding harder than ever. He knew whatever was waiting beyond the door wasn't ordinary, but his curiosity outweighed his fear.

Victor stood frozen for a moment, staring at the creepy door. The wind from inside was chilling, carrying whispers he couldn't quite make out. He took a deep breath, his hands trembling, and stepped in.

The door slammed shut behind him with a loud thud. He turned quickly, but it was too late. The door had vanished into the darkness, leaving him trapped in a space so dark it felt alive.

It was completely silent except for the sound of his heartbeat echoing in his ears.

"Hello? Is anyone there?" Victor's voice trembled as he called out. It bounced back to him, making him feel smaller and more alone.

He moved slowly, his hands stretched out to feel his way. The floor beneath him was cold and slightly wet, like it hadn't been touched for years. After a few hesitant steps, his hand brushed against something hard.

It was a wall, smooth and cold like ice. He pressed his hands flat against it, searching for a clue. Suddenly, glowing letters began to appear, as if the wall was alive. The light was dim at first, but it grew brighter, enough to make him squint.

The words glowed in an eerie green:
"The thirsty earthling blood."

Victor's body stiffened. His mind raced. Earthling? They know about Earth?

The word "thirsty" sent a chill down his spine. He whispered the words aloud, trying to understand. "Thirsty... earthling... blood?"

A wave of fear hit him. Was this place watching him? Did the creatures in this strange world crave humans? Was he their prey?

His breathing became shallow, but his curiosity pushed him forward. He needed to know what this meant. His fingers touched the chain around his neck—the one Clara had given him. It was a gift, something that always made him feel safe.

He unclasped it, staring at the small pendant attached to it. The edge of the pendant was sharp, like a tiny blade. He hesitated, then pressed it against the skin of his hand.

The sharp pain made him flinch, and a small drop of blood welled up from the scratch. It slid down his hand and hit the cold floor with a soft plop.

The moment the blood touched the ground, the wall in front of him began to shimmer. It cracked and crumbled, but instead of breaking into pieces, it dissolved into a strange, black mist.

Victor stepped back, startled, as the mist spread out, revealing an endless void. The room became colder, and a sound started to grow—at first a soft hum, then a loud roar.

Before he could react, water gushed out from the sides of the walls. It was icy cold, flooding the floor in seconds.

Victor panicked. "What is this? No! No!" he shouted, his voice drowned by the sound of rushing water.

He turned around, trying to find the door, but it was gone. There was nothing but smooth, wet walls all around him. The water rose quickly, reaching his knees, then his chest. It was freezing, making his body numb.

He slammed his fists against the walls, screaming for help, but no one answered. "Please! Somebody! Help me!"

The water reached his neck. He tried to stay afloat, but the space was too small. The icy water pressed against him, making it hard to breathe.

As the water covered his mouth, he gasped for air, but it was no use. It rose over his nose, his eyes, and finally his head. He was completely submerged.

Victor thrashed, his lungs burning, his mind screaming for air. His vision blurred, and his body grew heavy. Just before his eyes closed, he saw something glowing faintly in the water—the same words he'd read on the wall.

"The thirsty earthling blood."

The glow faded as his vision turned black. His body went limp, and the world around him disappeared into silence.

Victor's eyes fluttered open, his vision blurry. He felt something cold and slimy being thrown on his face. As he blinked, he saw a strange, red, furry creature staring at him with glowing yellow eyes. The creature's face was sharp, its teeth long, and its skin shimmered like it was wet.

Victor screamed in panic, but before he could make another sound, the creature clamped a heavy, furry hand over his mouth.

"Shhh!" the creature hissed in a voice that rumbled like thunder. It spoke words in a strange, guttural language that Victor couldn't understand.

Victor's heart pounded. His mind raced. What is this thing? Where am I? What's happening?

The creature tilted its head as if studying him. Then, without a word, it grabbed Victor by his arm and flung him over its shoulder like he weighed nothing.

"Hey! Put me down! What are you doing?" Victor yelled, but the creature ignored him.

It carried him through a dense jungle filled with glowing plants and strange, eerie sounds. The air was thick, and the ground squelched under the creature's heavy feet. Finally, they reached a clearing—a garden unlike anything Victor had ever seen.

The garden was alive with neon flowers and shimmering trees that seemed to hum softly. The ground glowed faintly, and a soft mist hung in the air. The creature threw Victor down onto the ground with a thud.

"Ouch! Can't you be a little gentle?" Victor groaned, rubbing his back.

The creature raised a furry finger to its mouth and hissed again. "Shhh!"

Victor fell silent, watching as the creature plucked a glowing, fluorescent plant from the garden. It crushed the plant in its massive hands, releasing a bright, sticky liquid. The creature then pulled out a small vial of some foul-smelling black liquid, mixed it with the plant juice, and swirled it together.

The mixture glowed brightly, casting eerie shadows across the garden. The creature turned to Victor, holding the strange concoction, and motioned for him to drink it.

Victor wrinkled his nose and shook his head. "No way. I'm not drinking that!"

The creature's eyes narrowed, and it let out a low growl. Suddenly, it opened its mouth wide, revealing sharp teeth, and blew out a small jet of fire. The flames danced in front of Victor's face, making him jump.

"Okay, okay! I'll drink it!" Victor said, holding up his hands in surrender.

He hesitated for a moment before taking the glowing mixture from the creature. The smell made his stomach turn, but he closed his eyes and gulped it down.

The liquid burned as it went down his throat, and he coughed violently. For a moment, everything felt wrong—his head spun, his ears rang, and his vision blurred.

But then, something strange happened. The creature spoke again in its odd, guttural language, and this time, Victor understood.

"Can you hear me now, earthling?" the creature asked, its voice deep and commanding.

Victor's eyes widened in shock. "Wait... I can understand you?"

The creature smirked, revealing its sharp teeth again. "Good. Now, we can talk."

Victor sat there, stunned. His mind was racing with questions. Who was this creature? What did it want? And how did it know he was from Earth?

Victor's mouth opened, and the questions poured out like water from a broken faucet.

"What is this place? Who are you? Why did you bring me here? What's with all the glowing plants? Why do you look like a giant red teddy bear with teeth? And why can I suddenly understand you?"

Gruffle's furry hand shot up, his yellow eyes narrowing. "STOP! You are pissing my head!"

Victor blinked, taken aback. "Pissing your head? I'm just asking—"

"Enough!" Gruffle growled, his deep voice echoing through the garden. He folded his arms, clearly annoyed. "I am Gruffle. And you, earthling, are in Drakoria."

Victor tilted his head. "Whatttt?" he said, his voice filled with disbelief.

Gruffle rolled his eyes and repeated himself slowly, enunciating each letter as if talking to a child. "You... are... in... Drakoria. D-R-A-K-O-R-I-A."

Victor raised his hands in exasperation. "I understand what you said, but what's Drakoria?!"

Gruffle sighed, his sharp teeth glinting as he began to explain. "Drakoria is a world unlike your Earth. It is a land of dragons, dinosaurs, and luminous life. Everything here is alive in ways you cannot imagine. The plants glow, the mountains breathe, and the sky burns with fire."

Victor's eyes widened as Gruffle continued.

"This world has two moons that control our tides and a fiery black sky that never changes. Creatures here are not like the ones on your Earth. They are bigger, stronger, and much smarter than you think. We do not live by your rules. Here, it's survival of the fittest. Even the plants can bite you if you're not careful."

Victor's jaw dropped. "Wait, did you say the plants can bite?"

"Yes!" Gruffle snapped. "And stop interrupting me! The luminous plants you see here give life to this world, but they also protect it. Touch the wrong one, and you might lose a finger—or worse."

Victor gulped, his hand instinctively moving away from a glowing flower nearby.

"Drakoria," Gruffle went on, "is a land divided. There are territories ruled by mighty dragons, dark forests where the shadows have eyes, and oceans so deep even the bravest don't dare to swim. Every corner of this world holds a mystery, and most of them are deadly."

Victor's mind spun as he tried to process everything. Dragons? Glowing plants? A sky that burns? It all sounded like something out of a fantasy novel.

"Why am I here?" Victor finally asked, his voice softer this time. "I mean, I didn't come here on purpose. The portal... it just pulled me in."

Gruffle leaned closer, his glowing eyes piercing into Victor's. "That," he said, "is the real question, earthling. Why are you here? And what does Drakoria want with you?"

Victor felt a chill run down his spine. The way Gruffle said it made it sound like this world was alive, like Drakoria itself had chosen him. But why? And what did it want from him?

Victor's curiosity got the better of him as they walked through the glowing forest. He kept firing questions at Gruffle, eager to know more about this strange, dangerous world.

"Gruffle, what are those glowing plants? Why does the sky look like fire? And why does this place feel like it's alive?"

Gruffle sighed heavily. "You ask too much, earthling. This world is not for the weak. Everything here—plants, skies, even the wind—has its purpose. Stop questioning and start surviving!"

As they moved forward, Victor felt something sharp under his foot. He yelped loudly, hopping on one leg. "Ouch! What the—what was that?"

He looked down and saw a spiky, cactus-like plant he had stepped on, its needles glowing faintly. The moment his voice echoed through the forest, everything around them fell silent. Then, out of nowhere, an eerie, whispering sound began. It was as if the trees, plants, and even the wind were speaking in hushed, haunting tones.

"What... what is that?" Victor stammered, his heart racing.

Gruffle's ears perked up, and his eyes widened in panic. "You fool! You've woken them!"

"Woken what?" Victor asked, but before he could get an answer, Gruffle grabbed him by the waist with one powerful arm and started running.

"Hold on, earthling!" Gruffle shouted, his voice trembling. He ran as fast as his legs could carry him, the forest around them alive with sinister whispers. The whispers grew louder, and strange shadows began to move in the glowing light.

Victor held on tightly, his head spinning. "What's happening? What did I wake up?"

Gruffle didn't answer. Instead, he started muttering something in a strange, guttural language, his voice low and urgent.

As the whispers turned into chilling wails, Gruffle reached the edge of a black, shimmering river. Without hesitation, he leaped into the dark water, diving deep with Victor still in his grasp.

Victor gasped as the cold water enveloped him. The river seemed endless, the light from above disappearing as they sank deeper. He felt Gruffle's strong grip guiding him through the murky depths.

Suddenly, Gruffle stopped and reached for something growing on the riverbed—two glowing, translucent leaves that pulsed with a faint blue light. He handed one to Victor and motioned for him to eat it.

Victor hesitated. "Eat this? Are you serious?"

Gruffle growled, his patience thinning. "Do it, or you will not survive!"

Reluctantly, Victor took a bite. The leaf tasted bitter, but as soon as he swallowed, the darkness around them seemed to shift. The cold, heavy water vanished, and Victor felt his body being pulled upward.

When he opened his eyes, he found himself inside a cozy, dimly lit cottage. The walls were made of rough stone, and strange glowing orbs hung from the ceiling, casting a warm, flickering light.

Gruffle stood nearby, shaking the water off his fur. "Welcome to my home," he said, his voice calmer now. "You're lucky we made it."

Victor looked around in awe. "How did we get here? What just happened?"

Gruffle smirked. "You stepped where you shouldn't have, earthling. This forest does not forgive trespassers. But now, you are safe... for the moment."

Victor sank into a strange, mossy chair, his mind racing. He had so many questions, but one thing was clear—Drakoria was far more dangerous than he had imagined.

4

Gruffle sat on a moss-covered chair, his glowing eyes fixed on Victor. The flickering light of the fire made his red fur seem even more ominous as he began his tale. His voice was low, like a distant rumble, as if the story itself carried the weight of centuries.

"Listen carefully, Earthling," Gruffle said, his tone both somber and urgent. "You need to understand the legends of Drakoria if you wish to survive here. Long ago, this world was different—a paradise of peace and harmony. We Drakorians were simple creatures, without magic or power. We lived off the luminous plants, the glowing rivers, and the fire-black skies. Each creature, from the smallest critter to the largest dinosaur, was content. There was no greed, no hatred, only kindness. Our leader, Drake, was the heart of our world. He was the embodiment of love and strength, keeping everything in balance."

Victor leaned in, captivated. "Drake... he sounds like a hero."

Gruffle nodded. "He was more than a hero. He was our lifeline. But he warned us—warned us that if hatred ever seeped into our hearts, it would bring ruin. At first, we ignored his words. How could such a peaceful world ever fall to darkness?" Gruffle's eyes darkened. "But hatred is like a spark. Small, but deadly. It began with jealousy, then anger, then betrayal. It spread like wildfire, consuming our paradise."

Victor shivered, the weight of the story pressing on him. "What happened next?"

Gruffle hesitated, then continued. "The obsidian compass appeared. No one knew where it came from, but it was ancient, powerful, and cursed. It opened a portal—a bridge between Drakoria and another world called the Damding Comsphere."

Victor's breath caught. "A portal? Like the one I came through?"

Gruffle nodded grimly. "Yes. But the portal didn't bring salvation. It brought invaders. The beings from Damding Comsphere were no ordinary creatures—they were shadows, masters of manipulation and greed. They whispered lies into the hearts of Drakorians, turning brother against brother, friend against friend. Even Drake, the strongest of us all, began to weaken. The balance he fought so hard to protect crumbled."

Victor's fists clenched. "And then?"

"Drake gave his life to protect us," Gruffle said, his voice heavy with sorrow. "His sacrifice sealed the portal, but it was too late. The invaders had already rooted themselves in our world. They pulled our entire existence into this twisted dimension—a warped version of the Drakoria we once knew. Now, this world belongs to them. They rule from the shadows, spreading their power across dimensions. Some Drakorians worship them, believing they saved us. But those like me..." Gruffle's eyes burned brighter. "We know the truth. They are the root of all evil. They destroyed our world and enslaved our spirits."

Victor was silent, his mind racing. "And the compass?" he asked finally.

Gruffle pointed a clawed finger at Victor. "The compass is the key. The obsidian compass connects worlds. It can open and close portals, bending reality itself. If it has called to you, then the Damding Comsphere already knows about you. They will come for you, Earthling. And they will stop at nothing to use the compass for their dark plans."

Victor swallowed hard, his heart pounding. "So... what do I do?"

Gruffle leaned closer, his face inches from Victor's. "You survive. And you fight. If you truly want to get back to your world, to your Clara, you must stop them. But be warned—the path ahead is filled with dangers you cannot imagine. The Damding Comsphere doesn't just destroy worlds; it devours souls."

Victor sat back, his thoughts swirling. The compass, the portals, the Damding Comsphere—it was all too much. But one thing was clear: he had stumbled into something far greater than himself. And now, there was no turning back.

Gruffle's voice dropped to a whisper, as if uttering the name itself could summon the entity. "There is one you must know of, Victor—the leader of the Damding Comsphere. His name is Noxmire."

Victor frowned. "Noxmire? Who is he?"

Gruffle's glowing eyes narrowed, his clawed fingers tracing circles in the air as if drawing the shape of something unseen. "Noxmire is the very opposite of Drake. Where Drake was the beacon of kindness, Noxmire is the embodiment of hatred, jealousy, and endless greed. Long before the portals, it is said he was a powerful being in his world, but his heart was consumed by the desire to control everything. His envy of other worlds, their peace, their prosperity—it drove him mad. And so, he sought a way to bridge worlds, to bring them all under his dominion."

Victor listened, his pulse quickening.

Gruffle continued, his tone grim. "That's when the obsidian compasses appeared. The source of their power is still a mystery, but every world—yours, mine, and countless others—has one. They are ancient, crafted from an energy not of this dimension. Each compass is a gateway, a key to connecting worlds. Noxmire learned to manipulate them, using their power to spread his reach. His goal is to conquer every realm, draining its essence, its life force, to fuel his own insatiable hunger for control."

Victor's eyes widened. "And he's using the compasses to do this?"

Gruffle nodded solemnly. "Yes. The compasses are bound to their worlds, and through them, Noxmire can open portals, create chaos, and enslave entire civilizations. It is said that he feeds off the despair and destruction he causes, growing stronger with each conquest. The Damding Comsphere is not just his empire; it is a fortress of worlds he has already destroyed, twisted into his dark vision."

Victor's stomach churned. The glowing compass he had collected in Carpathia suddenly felt heavier in his mind, as if its significance had doubled in an instant.

"But why me?" Victor asked. "Why did the compass call to me? I didn't ask for this!"

Gruffle's expression softened for a moment. "The compasses don't choose at random, Victor. They seek those with potential—those with the courage to resist, to fight. Perhaps the compass sensed something in you, something even you don't yet know."

Victor shook his head, overwhelmed. "But I'm just a man. How can I stop someone like Noxmire? How can I even survive in this place?"

Gruffle stood, his broad frame towering over Victor. "You are no ordinary man, Victor. You are here for a reason. The obsidian compass chose you, and with it, you might hold the key to something greater than you realize. But understand this: Noxmire is already aware of you now. By touching that compass, by stepping into the portal, you've marked yourself as a threat. He will come for you."

Victor's heart sank, but he clenched his fists. "Then I'll be ready."

Gruffle chuckled dryly. "Brave words for an Earthling. But bravery alone won't save you. If you wish to survive and find your way back to Clara, you'll need more than courage. You'll need allies, knowledge, and a strength you've never imagined. And if you truly want to stop Noxmire..." Gruffle's voice deepened ominously. "You'll need to find a way to destroy the obsidian compass itself."

Victor's mind reeled. Destroy the compass? The very thing that brought him here? How could he do that when he barely understood its power?

victor asked gruffle if any human had ever come before him. gruffle saud yes. Victor leaned in closer, his curiosity piqued. "Wait... another human? Someone from Earth like me? When did this happen?"

Gruffle nodded solemnly. "Yes, there was one. Long ago, my brother Brumble found him, just as I found you. That man was brave, perhaps braver than most. He was strong-willed and determined, even when we told him about Noxmire and the dangers of Drakoria."

Victor's mind raced with questions. "What happened to him? Did he escape? Did he find a way back?"

Gruffle's expression darkened, his glowing eyes flickering with an unreadable emotion. "He did manage to evade Noxmire. The Damding Comsphere hunted him relentlessly, using every trick and trap they could. But he was clever, resourceful. Through some unknown means, he escaped Noxmire's grasp."

Victor's heart lifted slightly. "So, he survived? Is he still here in Drakoria?"

Gruffle hesitated, looking conflicted. "No one truly knows. Some Drakorians whisper that he joined Noxmire, corrupted by promises of power and safety. Others believe he is still out there, hiding in the shadows, searching for answers. One thing is certain, Victor: in Drakoria, no one truly dies. Time works differently here. Life continues, but it's not the life you might know."

Victor shivered at the thought. "And this man, did he... leave anything behind? Anything that could help me?"

Gruffle stroked his chin, thinking deeply. "There were stories, Victor. Stories of him leaving behind maps, writings, clues—pieces of a larger puzzle. If those tales are true, they could lead to a way out of Drakoria... or to something even greater."

Victor's chest tightened with a mix of hope and unease. "What was his name?"

Gruffle shrugged. "He never told us. Or if he did, Brumble kept it to himself. But his courage, his determination—they were unforgettable. Perhaps his path and yours will cross, Victor. Or perhaps his fate will serve as a warning."

Victor stared at the floor, lost in thought. The idea of another human—a survivor, someone who might have faced the same trials—filled him with equal parts hope and dread. If this man could find a way to escape Noxmire's grasp, maybe he could too. But what if he had fallen, betrayed, or worse—become part of Noxmire's dark army?

Gruffle placed a heavy hand on Victor's shoulder. "You must tread carefully, Earthling. The choices you make here will echo far beyond Drakoria. And remember, Noxmire's eyes are everywhere."

Victor swallowed hard, his resolve tightening. "Then I'll have to be smarter, faster, and stronger than he expects."

Gruffle grinned faintly. "Brave words again. But bravery alone won't be enough. Now, rest, Victor. Tomorrow, we start preparing you for the journey ahead. The compass chose you for a reason, and we must uncover why."

Victor nodded, though his mind raced with endless questions. As he lay on the floor of Gruffle's modest cottage that night, he couldn't help but wonder: who was the mysterious human before him? And was he an ally... or another enemy waiting in the shadows?

victor couldn't sleep. he woke up Gruffle from a strange feeling and told that i know you know that human's name. Gruffle sighed and said "yes i know but i can't say it because noxmire can hear it and if he listened then he will search for me and i'll be vanished forever"

victor suggested if he could write it. Gruffle nodded and wrote the name on the wall. First victor couldn't understand what was written but then Gruffle sprinkled an slimy liquid and words seemed to understand. Victor saw and couldn't breathe for a moment. His eyes widened as he stared at the glowing letters on the wall: Max Morris Halloway. The name echoed in his mind like a distant thunderstorm.

"That's... that's my grandfather's name!" Victor whispered, his voice shaking. His chest felt tight, and a deep sense of dread started to creep into his heart.

Gruffle's fur bristled, and his glowing eyes turned a sharp shade of crimson. He grabbed Victor's shoulders and shook him, panic etched across his face. "You fool!" Gruffle growled. "You were not supposed to speak it out loud! Now

Noxmire knows. He can hear that name anywhere, anytime. He'll come for us!"

Victor stepped back, his legs trembling. "But how is it possible? My grandfather—he disappeared years ago. No one knows what happened to him. Why is his name here? What was he doing in Drakoria?"

Gruffle didn't answer immediately. Instead, he began pacing the room, muttering in a strange language and wringing his hands. He looked out the window nervously, as if expecting something to burst through at any moment.

Victor's voice rose in desperation. "Tell me, Gruffle! What does this mean? Why was he here? What did he do?!"

Gruffle stopped and turned sharply, his face dark with worry. "Your grandfather, Max Morris Halloway, came here long before you. He found a way through the portal, just like you did. But he wasn't just an Earthling—he was special. The compass chose him too. He... he was supposed to be the savior of Drakoria."

Victor blinked in confusion. "Savior? What are you talking about?"

Gruffle stepped closer, lowering his voice. "Drakoria's legends speak of an Earthling who would wield the obsidian compass to seal the portals forever, cutting off the Damding Comsphere and saving all worlds from Noxmire's reach. Your grandfather was that Earthling. He was brave and clever, but... something went wrong. He vanished before completing his mission. And now—" Gruffle hesitated, his voice trembling, "—now Noxmire believes you're here to finish what he started."

Victor's head spun. "Me? Why me? I didn't even know about this place until a few days ago!"

Gruffle pointed at the compass band on Victor's wrist. "The compass chose you, Victor. You carry the same bloodline, the same connection. Noxmire will think you're here to destroy him, just as your grandfather tried to. That name you spoke out loud—it's like lighting a beacon for him. He'll come for you now, and he won't stop until he has you."

Victor felt a cold sweat trickle down his neck. The room seemed to close in around him. "What do we do? How do we stop him from finding us?"

Gruffle grabbed a satchel from the corner of the room and started stuffing it with glowing plants and vials of strange liquids. "We run. We hide. And we figure out what your grandfather left behind. If he had a plan, we need to find it before Noxmire finds us."

As Gruffle pulled Victor toward the door, the cottage shook violently. A low, guttural growl echoed in the distance, growing louder by the second. The air grew heavy, and the faint smell of burning metal filled Victor's nostrils.

Gruffle froze, his eyes widening in terror. "He's here. Noxmire knows."

Victor's heart pounded as he looked at Gruffle. "What do we do now?"

Gruffle tightened his grip on Victor's arm. "We survive. For now."

Without another word, Gruffle dragged Victor out of the cottage and into the darkness of the glowing forest, the haunting growls of their pursuer echoing behind them.

As soon as Victor uttered the name "Max Morris Halloway," the entire world seemed to shift. The skies turned an ominous shade of fiery black, and deafening thunder rumbled across Drakoria. Bright streaks of lightning split the sky, and a chilling wind swept through the forest. Flames erupted sporadically in the sky, casting an eerie glow over everything. It was as if the entire realm was warning them—evil had been awakened.

Gruffle's eyes widened in pure terror. "You shouldn't have said that name!" he growled, grabbing Victor by the arm. "Now they know! Now he knows!"

Victor's heart pounded as the air around them grew colder. He could feel the weight of something sinister closing in. "What's happening?" he stammered, his voice trembling.

"No time to explain!" Gruffle snapped. He yanked Victor toward a small, bubbling pond nearby. The water shimmered with an unnatural, slimy texture. Gruffle muttered something quickly in his native tongue and then scooped up a handful of the slimy liquid. "Drink!" he ordered, his tone urgent.

Victor hesitated, but the look in Gruffle's glowing eyes left no room for argument. He pinched his nose and gulped down the slimy water, gagging slightly as it slid down his throat. Gruffle did the same.

Within seconds, Victor felt his body tingle, and the world around them blurred. It was as though they were being sucked through a tunnel of swirling colors. A loud, whistling sound filled Victor's ears, and his stomach flipped.

When the world stopped spinning, they were inside a cozy but cluttered house. The walls were lined with strange glowing artifacts, and the air smelled faintly of herbs and smoke. Standing in the middle of the room was another creature—a slightly smaller version of Gruffle but with darker fur and piercing green eyes.

The creature, clearly startled, let out a low growl. "A human? Here? Gruffle, what have you done?"

Gruffle raised his hands defensively. "Calm down, Brumble! This is Victor. He is... he is the grandson of Max Morris Halloway."

Brumble's expression shifted instantly from alarm to astonishment. He took a step closer, his glowing green eyes scanning Victor from head to toe. "The grandson of Max?" he repeated, his voice filled with wonder.

Victor blinked, still trying to process everything. "Wait, you know my grandfather?"

Brumble let out a booming laugh, puffing out his chest proudly. "Of course I do! Max Morris Halloway was no ordinary human. He was a legend here in Drakoria. If you are his blood, then you have great power within you."

Victor frowned, confusion etched on his face. "I don't feel powerful. I just want answers. What happened to him? Why am I here?"

Brumble placed a heavy paw on Victor's shoulder, his grip surprisingly gentle. "All in good time, young one. But first, let me say this: if you are anything like your grandfather, then perhaps there is hope for us after all."

Victor's eyes darted nervously between Gruffle and Brumble as the weight of their words sank in. "But… you both just said his name. Won't Noxmire hear us now? Won't he know where we are?" he asked, his voice trembling slightly.

Gruffle gave a quick, reassuring nod. "Not yet," he said, his tone serious. "Right now, we're inside Blackeye."

Victor tilted his head in confusion. "Blackeye? What's that?"

Brumble stepped forward, his green eyes glowing softly in the dim light of the cottage. "Blackeye is a safe circle," he explained. "It's a powerful, temporary shield that hides us from Noxmire and his spies. While we're inside, they can't trace us or hear anything we say. But…"

"But what?" Victor asked, feeling his heart race.

Gruffle sighed heavily and gestured toward the glowing runes on the floor, which were slowly dimming. "But it doesn't last long," he said grimly. "When the Blackeye fades, they'll know where we are again. That's why we must work fast, Victor. We don't have much time."

Victor glanced at the fading runes, the urgency in their voices making his chest tighten. "What do we need to do? What can I do to help?"

Brumble exchanged a glance with Gruffle, then stepped closer to Victor. "First, you need to understand who your grandfather was and why you're here. Max wasn't just a brave human; he was the first earthling to discover the obsidian compass and its connection to Drakoria. He saw what Noxmire was doing—how he was tearing apart worlds to grow his power. Max… he tried to stop him."

Victor's breath hitched. "Tried to stop him? What happened to him?"

Brumble's gaze softened, a mix of admiration and sorrow in his expression. "Max fought harder than anyone. But Noxmire is not easily defeated. Some say Max escaped, hiding in a dimension where even Noxmire can't reach him. Others believe he's still here, working in the shadows. The truth is, no one knows for sure. But one thing is clear: Noxmire feared him. And now, he will fear you too."

Victor felt a strange mix of pride and fear at those words. "Me? I don't even know what I'm doing here! How can I possibly stop someone like Noxmire?"

Gruffle placed a paw on Victor's shoulder, his grip firm. "Because you have something Max had—a connection to the obsidian compass. It brought you here for a reason. You're not just here by accident, Victor. You're part of something much bigger."

Victor swallowed hard, his mind racing. The glowing runes on the floor were now barely visible, their light flickering like a dying flame. He could feel the tension in the room growing thicker by the second.

"What do we do now?" Victor asked, his voice barely above a whisper.

Brumble straightened, his green eyes blazing with determination. "We move fast. We find the next clue before Noxmire's forces catch up to us. And we keep you alive, no matter what."

As the last glow of the Blackeye faded, a low, ominous rumble shook the cottage. Gruffle's fur bristled, and Brumble's eyes darted toward the door.

"They're coming," Gruffle muttered. "Victor, stay close. This is just the beginning."

Victor's heart pounded as he prepared to follow them, stepping into the unknown once more.

Victor was trembling, his eyes wide with fear as he watched the shadows creeping closer, dark and menacing, almost alive. The Blackeye shield was fading fast, and he could feel the cold, eerie presence of the black shadows pressing in around them.

Gruffle and Brumble exchanged a determined look, their faces steeled with resolve. Gruffle turned to Victor and placed a firm paw on his shoulder. "Stay inside, no matter what," he instructed, his voice low but commanding.

Victor nodded, too scared to argue. He watched as Gruffle and Brumble stepped outside, their silhouettes barely visible in the swirling darkness.

The two Drakorians stood side by side, their furry hands clasped tightly together. They began chanting in a strange, echoing language that made Victor's skin crawl. The air around them grew heavy, vibrating with energy, and their eyes glowed fiercely.

With a final, synchronized motion, Gruffle and Brumble lifted their hands high, and then thrust them forward. A blinding flash of lightning erupted from their palms, accompanied by a deafening crack of thunder. The bolt shot straight into the shadows, ripping through them like a storm tearing apart a dark sky.

The shadows screamed—a bone-chilling sound that made Victor cover his ears—and began to dissolve, retreating into the nothingness from which they had come. In their place, a shimmering, frozen shield formed, encasing Gruffle, Brumble, and Victor in a protective barrier of crystalline ice.

Gruffle turned, his face slick with sweat, and yelled, "Victor! Now!"

Without hesitation, Gruffle and Brumble grabbed Victor by the arms, pulling him with them as they ran toward the slimy black liquid river. The ground beneath them rumbled, and the air crackled with tension as the last remnants of the shadows clawed at the edges of the frozen shield.

They reached the river just as the shield began to crack. Gruffle handed Victor a handful of the slimy liquid and gestured for him to drink. "Quick! No time to waste!"

Victor gagged at the smell but obeyed, swallowing the strange liquid in one gulp. Brumble and Gruffle did the same.

In the blink of an eye, the three of them were no longer surrounded by darkness or shadows. The air cleared, and Victor realized they were back in Gruffle's warm, cozy house.

Victor stumbled and fell onto the floor, gasping for breath. His heart was pounding so hard it felt like it might burst out of his chest. He looked up at Gruffle and Brumble, both of whom were leaning against the wall, panting heavily.

"What... what just happened?" Victor asked, his voice shaking.

Gruffle wiped his brow and gave Victor a weak smile. "We bought ourselves some time," he said. "But it won't last long. Noxmire's forces are stronger than ever. We'll have to be ready for what comes next."

Victor nodded slowly, his fear slowly giving way to a newfound determination. He knew now that he was in the middle of something far bigger than himself—and that there was no turning back.

Gruffle, Brumble, and Victor were sitting in silence, thinking about what to do next. Suddenly, a loud BANG broke through the stillness. All three of them jumped to their feet, alarmed.

"What was that?" Victor whispered, his heart racing.

They ran outside, following the sound. There was rustling in the bushes, and something—or someone—was crawling out. Victor's breath caught in his chest as he saw her.

Clara.

Victor froze for a second, unable to believe his eyes. "Clara?" he whispered. Then, without thinking, he ran to her and hugged her tightly.

"What are you doing here? How did you get here?" he asked, his voice shaking with emotion.

But Clara didn't hug him back. She pulled away, her face full of tears and anger. "I hate you, Victor!" she shouted. "Why did you leave me? Why didn't you tell me anything?"

Victor stood stunned, guilt washing over him. "Clara, I—"

"You just disappeared!" Clara cried. "You left a stupid note and went into danger all alone! Do you know how scared I was? I thought I'd never see you again!"

Victor tried to explain, his voice soft. "Clara, I didn't want to put you in danger. I thought it was safer if you stayed behind."

"Safer?" Clara said, her voice trembling. "How could you think I'd just sit there and do nothing? When you and that compass went missing, I followed the traces. I followed the signal, Victor! I found the same Carpathian compass shop, the same portal, and it brought me here!"

Victor's heart sank as he realized what she'd been through. "Clara... I'm so sorry. I didn't know you'd—"

"You didn't know because you didn't even think about me!" Clara shouted, fresh tears streaming down her face. "Do you have any idea how scared I was, not knowing if you were alive? I thought... I thought I lost you forever!"

Victor reached for her hands, his voice breaking. "Clara, I'm sorry. I was wrong. I shouldn't have left you. I never wanted to hurt you."

Clara stared at him, her tears slowing down but her voice still shaking. "Victor, I couldn't let you go. I love you too much to just stay behind. I didn't care about the danger. I had to find you."

Victor hugged her again, this time more tightly, as if he'd never let go. "I love you too, Clara. I'm so sorry. I promise I'll never leave you again."

Behind them, Gruffle and Brumble watched silently, their faces serious. Brumble finally spoke. "Victor, if she followed the compass, Noxmire might know about her now too. We need to move fast."

Victor nodded, still holding Clara. He looked into her eyes and said, "We're in this together now. I won't let anything happen to you."

Clara wiped her tears, her voice firm. "Good. Because I'm not leaving your side, no matter what happens."

The four of them stood there, knowing the danger was far from over, but for the first time in a while, Victor felt a small glimmer of hope. They were together, and together, they would face whatever came next.

The four of them went back into the cottage, where Clara sat down, her face pale and full of questions. Victor handed her some water and asked gently, "Clara, tell us everything. How did you get here?"

Clara took a deep breath, still shaken. "After you disappeared, I found the note you left, Victor. I was so angry, but I knew I couldn't just sit and wait. I went to your lab and saw the compass you'd brought from the Carpathian shop was missing. I had a feeling it was connected to your disappearance, so I went back to the shop."

She paused, her voice trembling. "When I got there, it looked... different. Darker, like something had changed. I found a door in the back, the same one you must have opened. I saw strange carvings and a statue with an eye and a foot. I figured out how to open the door, and when I did, the portal appeared. I didn't think—I just stepped in, hoping it would lead me to you. Next thing I knew, I was here."

Gruffle sighed deeply, his expression grim. "This is bad. Very bad."

"What do you mean?" Clara asked, looking worried.

Gruffle's tone was serious. "The more humans that enter Drakoria, the stronger the connection becomes between this world and yours. Noxmire thrives on this. It makes it easier for him to track us and break through the barriers that keep him out of other worlds. Your presence here... it accelerates everything."

Clara's eyes widened, and she looked at Victor. "Victor, what have we done?"

Victor squeezed her hand. "Clara, it's not your fault. If anyone's to blame, it's me. But now that you're here, we'll figure this out together."

Gruffle and Brumble exchanged glances, and Brumble spoke up. "She needs to know everything. There's no time for secrets anymore."

Gruffle nodded and began explaining. "Clara, this world, Drakoria, wasn't always like this. It was a land of peace, ruled by Drake, a leader of kindness and balance. But when hatred spread, the obsidian compass opened a portal to another world—the Damding Comsphere. That world's leader, Noxmire, is the opposite of Drake. He's full of jealousy and hatred, and he wants to conquer every world using the obsidian compass. He destroys, enslaves, and consumes everything in his path."

Victor added, "Noxmire's forces pulled Drakoria into their chaos, trapping everyone here. My grandfather, Max Morris Halloway, was the only other human to come here. He tried to fight back but disappeared. Some say he's still hiding, looking for a way to stop Noxmire, but no one knows for sure."

Clara listened quietly, her face pale as she tried to take it all in. "So... we're stuck in a world ruled by a monster, and he's after us now because of the compass?"

"Yes," Gruffle said. "And now that you're here, we have even less time. The balance is tipping in Noxmire's favor."

Clara took a deep breath, trying to steady herself. "This is... a lot. But what do we do now? How do we stop him?"

Brumble stood tall, his voice firm. "We fight back. If your grandfather is still alive, he might have answers. But to find him, we'll need to move quickly. Every moment we stay here, Noxmire gets closer."

Victor looked at Clara, his voice full of determination. "Clara, I know this is terrifying, but I'm not letting anything happen to you. We'll face this together."

Clara nodded, her eyes brimming with both fear and resolve. "I'm with you. Whatever it takes, we'll figure this out."

Gruffle and Brumble looked at each other and then at the two humans. "We need to prepare," Gruffle said. "The battle ahead won't be easy. But if we stand together, there's still hope."

And with that, the four of them began planning their next move, knowing the clock was ticking and the fight for Drakoria—and perhaps all worlds—had truly begun.

Victor turned to Gruffle and Brumble with urgency in his voice. "Isn't there any place where Noxmire's forces can't find us? Somewhere safer?"

Gruffle scratched his chin thoughtfully, but it was Brumble who spoke up. "There is one place... the Holy Drake Palace. It's said to be the only place in Drakoria where Noxmire's power cannot penetrate. The palace is shielded by the essence of Drake himself, but..."

"But what?" Victor pressed.

Brumble sighed. "No one has ever managed to enter. The gates are locked by a powerful enchantment, and to unlock them, you need to pour something into the Holy Cup of Drake. The problem is... no one knows what that something is. The only clue is a riddle inscribed at the palace gates."

Victor leaned forward, intrigued. "A riddle? What does it say?"

Brumble hesitated. "It goes like this:
'From the heart of the lost,
By the light of the first flame,
The gift of truth shall unlock,
And the path to kindness reclaim.'

Many have tried to solve it, but none have succeeded. The palace remains sealed, untouched for centuries."

Clara, listening intently, said, "If it's the safest place, we should at least try. We can't just sit here waiting for Noxmire to catch us."

Victor nodded in agreement. "She's right. We have to go. Maybe we'll figure out the riddle when we're there. What do we have to lose?"

Gruffle looked uneasy. "It's not just about solving the riddle. The journey to the Holy Drake Palace is dangerous. It's hidden deep within the Luminous Spires, and the path is guarded by creatures loyal to Noxmire. And even if we get there, failing to unlock the palace might alert him to our presence."

Victor's voice was steady. "Then we don't fail. Clara and I didn't come all this way to give up now. We'll face whatever comes together."

Brumble sighed, a mix of admiration and worry in his expression. "You humans are either incredibly brave or incredibly foolish. But perhaps... you're the change we've been waiting for."

Gruffle, though hesitant, finally nodded. "Very well. If you're determined, we'll guide you to the Holy Drake Palace. But know this: once we begin, there's no turning back."

Clara squeezed Victor's hand, her determination matching his. "We're ready. Let's go."

With that, the group began their preparations, knowing the journey ahead would test not only their strength but their hearts and minds as well. The Holy Drake Palace awaited, and with it, the hope of salvation—or the shadow of failure.

Brumble and Gruffle exchanged serious glances before making a decision. Brumble spoke first. "If we're going to reach the Holy Drake Palace safely, we'll need protection. Noxmire's forces will stop at nothing to find us, and we can't risk going unprepared."

Gruffle nodded and added, "We have a small group of trusted allies. They've resisted Noxmire for years and are skilled in combat. I'll summon them. They'll shield us on our journey."

Within a short time, a group of ten Drakorian warriors arrived, each clad in luminous armor that seemed to hum with an otherworldly energy. They bowed slightly to Gruffle and Brumble, acknowledging their leadership. One of them, a tall Drakorian with glowing green scales named Zaron, stepped forward. "We're ready to protect you with our lives," he said firmly.

Victor and Clara felt a mix of awe and gratitude as they saw the warriors assemble. Clara whispered to Victor, "I hope we're not leading them into danger they can't handle."

Victor squeezed her hand. "We'll do our part, Clara. They believe in this, just like we have to."

The group set out into the Drake Forest, a place that seemed alive with energy. The air was thick with glowing spores that floated like fireflies, and the trees had trunks that twisted unnaturally, their bark shimmering with hues of blue and silver.

Brumble walked at the front, his eyes scanning the path ahead. Gruffle stayed near Victor and Clara, explaining their plan in a low voice. "Noxmire's army wears special Obsidian Bands. These bands allow them to bypass many of the traps and barriers in the forest. If we can manage to take a few of those bands, we'll stand a better chance of reaching the palace without detection."

Victor frowned. "And how do we get those bands? Just ask nicely?"

Gruffle smirked. "Not quite. We'll have to ambush a small patrol. Noxmire's forces scout these woods regularly, but they usually travel in groups of three or four. If we're quick, we can overpower them before they alert others."

Clara shuddered at the thought of a fight but steeled herself. "If it's what we need to do, then let's do it."

As they ventured deeper into the forest, Brumble raised a hand, signaling the group to stop. He whispered, "There. Ahead."

Victor and Clara squinted through the dense trees and saw them—three of Noxmire's soldiers. They were tall, hunched figures with sharp, insect-like features, their glowing red eyes scanning the forest. Each wore a black band on their forearms, pulsating with a faint light.

Zaron leaned close to Gruffle. "Let me and my warriors handle this. Stay back with the humans."

Before Victor could protest, Zaron and two other warriors slipped into the shadows. They moved with practiced precision, their luminous armor dimming to blend with the surroundings.

The ambush was swift. Zaron leaped from a tree, striking the first soldier with a glowing spear. The second warrior silenced another with a quick blow, while the third grappled the last soldier, pinning them to the ground.

It was over in seconds. Victor and Clara barely had time to process what had happened when Zaron returned, holding the three Obsidian Bands.

"These should do," he said, handing them to Gruffle.

Gruffle inspected the bands and nodded. "Good work. Let's keep moving before more of them show up."

As they ventured deeper into the forest, Brumble raised a hand, signaling the group to stop. He whispered, "There. Ahead."

Victor and Clara squinted through the dense trees and saw them—three of Noxmire's soldiers. They were tall, hunched figures with sharp, insect-like features, their glowing red eyes scanning the forest. Each wore a black band on their forearms, pulsating with a faint light.

Zaron leaned close to Gruffle. "Let me and my warriors handle this. Stay back with the humans."

Before Victor could protest, Zaron and two other warriors slipped into the shadows. They moved with practiced precision, their luminous armor dimming to blend with the surroundings.

The ambush was swift. Zaron leaped from a tree, striking the first soldier with a glowing spear. The second warrior silenced another with a quick blow, while the third grappled the last soldier, pinning them to the ground.

It was over in seconds. Victor and Clara barely had time to process what had happened when Zaron returned, holding the three Obsidian Bands.

"These should do," he said, handing them to Gruffle.

Gruffle inspected the bands and nodded. "Good work. Let's keep moving before more of them show up."

Brumble carefully handed the Obsidian Bands to Victor, Clara, and Gruffle, his expression serious. "These bands will disguise your energy signature, making it harder for Noxmire's forces to detect you. But remember, they're not foolproof. If you act suspiciously or attract too much attention, the bands won't protect you."

Victor examined the band closely. It felt cold and oddly heavy in his hand, like it was pulsing faintly with life. "How do we activate it?" he asked.

Brumble pointed to a small, glowing rune on the inside of the band. "Touch this rune, and the band will bind itself to you. You'll feel a slight sting, but that means it's working."

Clara hesitated, looking at the band with a mix of apprehension and curiosity. "And... this won't harm us, right?"

Gruffle chuckled softly. "It won't harm you, but it might make you feel a little strange at first. Just put it on, human."

Victor slid the band onto his wrist and pressed the rune. A sharp, stinging sensation shot up his arm, and for a moment, his vision blurred. When it cleared, he noticed a faint, shadowy aura surrounding him. Clara and Gruffle did the same, each reacting similarly as the bands activated.

Brumble nodded in approval. "Good. Now, listen carefully. These bands will only last a few hours before their energy fades. Move quickly and stay together. I'll gather more bands for my warriors and follow you from behind. Head toward the Crimson Veil, the boundary of the Drake Forest. Once you cross it, you'll be on the final path to the Holy Drake Palace."

Clara looked worried. "But why aren't you coming with us now?"

Brumble placed a reassuring hand on her shoulder. "If I leave without ensuring the rest of my warriors are prepared, we won't stand a chance if Noxmire's army catches up. Trust me, I'll find you before you reach the palace."

Victor nodded reluctantly. "Alright, Brumble. We'll trust your plan. Just... don't take too long."

Brumble gave a faint smile. "I'll be right behind you. Now go."

The Journey Continues

Victor, Clara, and Gruffle moved cautiously through the dense forest, their steps silent under Brumble's guidance. The eerie beauty of the forest felt heavier now, the luminous flora casting long, flickering shadows as they progressed.

Gruffle kept a keen eye on their surroundings, his voice low as he muttered, "The Crimson Veil isn't far, but it's heavily guarded. These bands should get us past the outer defenses, but we'll still need to be careful."

Victor glanced at Clara, who was gripping his arm tightly. "Are you okay?" he asked softly.

Clara nodded, though her face betrayed her nerves. "I'm fine. Just... don't let go of my hand."

Victor squeezed her hand reassuringly. "I won't."

Approaching the Crimson Veil

As they neared the Crimson Veil, a strange red mist began to fill the air. The trees became sparser, replaced by jagged rocks that glowed faintly in the dark. The ground beneath their feet felt brittle, cracking slightly with each step.

Gruffle paused, holding up a hand to signal them to stop. "This is it. The Crimson Veil," he whispered.

Victor peered through the mist and saw faint silhouettes moving—Noxmire's scouts. They were patrolling the area, their glowing red eyes scanning the terrain.

Clara swallowed hard. "How do we get past them?"

Gruffle motioned to their bands. "Stay calm. Walk steadily and confidently, but don't look directly at them. The bands will do the rest. If we hesitate or panic, they'll sense us."

Victor nodded, pulling Clara close. "We'll be fine. Just stay with me."

With a deep breath, they stepped into the mist, their hearts pounding as the silhouettes grew clearer. The scouts were tall and menacing, their insect-like forms glistening under the faint red glow of the Veil. One of them paused, its head tilting slightly as if sensing something.

Victor held his breath, his grip on Clara tightening. But the scout turned away after a moment, continuing its patrol.

They moved steadily, each step feeling like an eternity, until they finally emerged on the other side of the Veil. The air felt lighter, though the tension remained.

Gruffle exhaled deeply. "We made it. But we're not safe yet. Let's keep moving."

Victor and Clara exchanged a relieved glance but knew the real challenge was still ahead—the Holy Drake Palace and the mystery it held.

Gruffle, Clara, and Victor stood frozen when the soldier said, "Good luck, humans."

Victor's heart sank. "He knows!"

Before they could think, Gruffle roared and shot fire from his hand, burning the soldier into ash. But it was too late. A loud horn blasted through the air, shaking the ground. Strange cries and growls came from all around.

"RUN!" Gruffle shouted, pulling Victor and Clara forward.

They ran as fast as they could, the sound of heavy footsteps and clicking claws chasing after them. Clara stumbled, but Victor grabbed her arm.

"Don't stop!" he yelled.

Gruffle turned back, throwing fireballs at the shadowy figures closing in. They were noxmire soldiers—creatures with sharp claws, glowing red eyes, and twisted, insect-like bodies.

"They've found us!" Gruffle growled.

Victor shouted, "What do we do now?"

"We keep moving!" Gruffle snapped.

Suddenly, the ground ended. They stood at the edge of a giant cliff, staring down into a glowing ravine. The light shimmered like fire, and sharp rocks waited below.

"We're trapped!" Clara cried.

Gruffle pointed to a narrow bridge made of twisting roots and vines stretching across the ravine. It swayed dangerously in the wind.

"That's our way!" Gruffle said.

Victor stared at it. "That's not a bridge; that's a death trap!"

"Do you want to stay here and die?" Gruffle shot back.

Behind them, the soldiers were getting closer. Gruffle blasted another fireball at the group, sending them scattering.

"Move now!" Gruffle yelled.

Victor and Clara stepped onto the bridge, their legs shaking as it swayed beneath them.

"Don't look down!" Victor said, gripping Clara's hand.

The bridge creaked and groaned under their weight. Halfway across, the vines began snapping one by one.

"Hurry!" Gruffle shouted, still throwing fire at the soldiers.

Victor and Clara reached the other side just as the bridge gave way. Gruffle jumped, landing with a thud beside them.

The soldiers stopped at the edge of the cliff, snarling and pacing, unable to cross.

Clara collapsed to the ground, breathing heavily. "Are we safe now?"

Gruffle shook his head. "No. They'll find another way. We have to keep moving."

They ran again, the glowing towers of the Holy Drake Palace shining in the distance like a beacon.

"What happens when we get there?" Clara asked, her voice trembling.

Gruffle didn't answer. His face looked grim. "We'll figure it out when we get inside."

Victor turned to Clara. "Stay close to me. We'll get through this."

The air around them grew heavy, and Victor felt a strange pull toward the palace. It was as if the ground itself was leading them.

As they approached the palace gates, a loud roar came from behind. The soldiers had found another path and were closing in fast.

Gruffle stopped, his hand glowing with fire. "Go inside! I'll hold them off!"

Victor grabbed Gruffle's arm. "No! We need you!"

Gruffle hesitated, then growled, "Fine! But we have to move now!"

They reached the palace gates. Suddenly, the ground beneath them shook violently, and the gates opened by themselves.

Victor looked at Clara. "Are you ready?"

She nodded, fear in her eyes. "Let's do this together."

As they stepped inside, the gates slammed shut behind them, and everything went dark.

The only thing they could hear was a low, eerie whisper echoing in the air: "Welcome to the end."

Gruffle's voice echoed through the eerie silence. "Who are you, and what do you want?"

The whisper returned, cold and sharp. "I am Grivi, daughter of Noxmire. And I want the humans," she said, followed by a chilling, evil laugh that sent shivers down Victor and Clara's spines.

Gruffle growled, his fists glowing faintly with fire. "How did you get here?"

Grivi's voice sneered. "Why should I tell you? Foolish creatures. You think you can escape my father's reach?"

Suddenly, the air grew heavy, and an ominous red light filled the room. The source was a glass ball hanging in mid-air, pulsating with dark energy. Grivi's laughter grew louder, vibrating through the walls.

Victor clutched Clara's hand tightly. "What is happening?"

Gruffle snarled. "She's trying to trap us with her dark power."

But before anyone could react, a deafening crash echoed through the chamber. A powerful force shattered the glass ball into tiny shards, sending a shockwave that knocked everyone off their feet.

When Victor opened his eyes, he saw Brumble standing tall, his hands glowing with pure, golden light. His face was stern, and his presence felt like a shield against the darkness.

"I told you I'd protect you," Brumble said, his voice steady.

Gruffle smiled weakly. "Just in time, brother."

Grivi's voice screeched from the broken shards. "You dare defy me?"

Brumble ignored her, raising his hands to create a glowing barrier around the group. But before the barrier could fully form, a surge of dark energy burst forth from the broken ball, engulfing everyone.

Victor felt his body grow cold, his vision fading as the dark energy wrapped around them like a thick fog. He could barely hear Clara calling his name, her voice faint and distant.

Everything went black.

Victor's mind spun, and for a moment, he felt like he was floating in an endless void. Whispers filled the silence, voices he couldn't understand. Then, one voice rose above the rest—it was Grivi again, cruel and mocking.

"You cannot run from us. This is only the beginning."

Victor jolted awake, gasping for air. He found himself lying on a cold, stone floor. Around him were Clara, Gruffle, and Brumble, all slowly regaining consciousness. The room was different now—darker, colder, and filled with an unsettling silence.

"What just happened?" Clara asked, her voice trembling.

Gruffle rubbed his head. "That was her—Grivi's power. She's stronger than I thought."

Brumble stood up, his face pale. "She's trying to weaken us, to make us vulnerable. We have to keep moving before she strikes again."

Victor helped Clara to her feet. "Where are we now?"

Gruffle looked around, his eyes narrowing. "Still in the palace... but something's changed."

The walls of the palace glowed faintly with red symbols, pulsing like a heartbeat. It felt alive, as if the building itself was watching them.

Brumble looked at Victor. "We have to find the holy cup before it's too late. Grivi and her father won't stop until they have you."

Victor nodded, determination in his eyes. "Then let's not waste any more time."

The group moved forward, stepping deeper into the unknown, with the feeling that something—or someone—was waiting for them.

The group spread out through the eerie, glowing chamber, each of them searching desperately for the Holy Cup. The walls pulsed with crimson symbols, and the air was thick with tension. Victor's heart raced as he scanned every corner, the urgency gnawing at him.

Suddenly, Clara's voice pierced the silence. "I found it!"

Everyone turned toward her voice and ran to her side. Clara stood near an ancient pedestal, her face illuminated by the faint golden glow of a magnificent, ornate cup. The Holy Cup was encrusted with strange runes and shimmered as if alive.

Brumble approached cautiously, his eyes wide. "Yes... that's it. The Holy Cup. The key to the Drake Palace."

Gruffle exhaled deeply, relief mixed with unease. "But it's not just about finding it. We need to solve the riddle before we can use it."

Victor peered at the pedestal. A carved inscription glowed faintly beneath the cup. He read it aloud:

"What flows without end, gives life and binds,
Yet taken alone, destruction it finds.
Pour the gift, and the path shall be clear.
Fail, and darkness will draw ever near."

The group exchanged nervous glances.

Clara whispered, "What does it mean? 'Flows without end'? Is it water?"

Brumble shook his head. "No. The riddle says it binds and gives life. Water alone doesn't fit the last line—it's something more."

Victor's brow furrowed. "Something that gives life... but also destroys if taken alone?"

Gruffle rubbed his chin thoughtfully. "It must be something essential, something tied to life itself."

Clara's voice trembled. "What about blood?"

The room fell silent.

Victor's eyes widened. "Blood... it flows endlessly within us. It gives life, binds families, and can destroy if spilled."

Brumble nodded solemnly. "It makes sense. But pouring blood into the Holy Cup... it's dangerous. The cup might demand more than just a drop."

Gruffle looked at Victor. "You're the one tied to this journey, Victor. The compass, your grandfather—it's all connected to you. The choice is yours."

Victor swallowed hard, staring at the Holy Cup. He felt Clara's hand on his shoulder. "Are you sure about this?" she asked softly, her eyes full of worry.

Victor nodded slowly. "If this is the only way to move forward, I'll do it. For all of us."

He took a deep breath, removed the sharp pendant from Clara's necklace, and made a small cut on his palm. A few drops of blood dripped into the Holy Cup, and the glowing runes flared brighter.

Suddenly, the ground beneath them rumbled. The cup absorbed the blood, and the symbols on the walls began to shift and rearrange, forming a new passage.

Brumble whispered, "You solved it. The path to the Drake Palace is opening."

Gruffle looked around nervously. "We need to move fast. Grivi and Noxmire will feel this. They'll know where we are."

Victor clenched his fist, steeling himself. "Then let's go. We don't have time to waste."

With the newly revealed path glowing ahead of them, the group stepped forward into the unknown, each of them knowing they were walking deeper into danger—and closer to the truth.

As they stepped into the newly revealed path, a lingering question hung heavy in the air. Clara was the first to voice it. "Why was the riddle different? Weren't you expecting this one?"

Gruffle and Brumble exchanged glances before Brumble spoke, his voice steady yet thoughtful. "The riddle... it changes. The words may be different for each who seeks to solve it, but the answer remains the same."

Victor frowned. "But if the answer has always been blood, why hasn't anyone ever solved it before?"

Brumble sighed deeply. "Because, Victor, none of us here—no Drakorian—has blood. We're creatures of energy, of form, but not of flesh and blood like you humans. That's why the Holy Cup has remained sealed for all these ages. Without blood, it could never be opened."

Clara's eyes widened as the realization sank in. "So... my grandfather... Max Morris Halloway... if he's alive—"

Brumble cut in, his voice filled with a cautious hope. "Then he's most likely inside the Drake Palace. It's the only place where noxmire's forces can't reach. If Max solved the riddle as you just did, he might've entered and stayed there all this time."

Victor's breath caught in his throat. His grandfather—his long-lost link to the mysteries of Drakoria and the compass—might be just ahead. But the thought was bittersweet.

"If he's inside," Victor said slowly, "why didn't he come back? Why did he leave us wondering all these years?"

Brumble's expression turned somber. "The Drake Palace is a place of ultimate protection, yes, but it's also a prison of sorts. The shield that keeps noxmire out... it also locks everything within. If your grandfather is there, he couldn't leave, even if he wanted to."

Gruffle nodded. "The palace is not just a sanctuary—it's a last stand. Whoever enters must be ready to face the secrets and the sacrifices it holds."

Victor clenched his fists, his determination solidifying. "Then we need to get there. If my grandfather is alive, we'll find him. We'll finish what he started."

Brumble placed a reassuring hand on Victor's shoulder. "We'll stand with you. But be prepared, Victor. The Drake Palace holds truths that can shatter even the strongest hearts. Whatever lies beyond that door will test you more than anything you've faced so far."

Clara grabbed Victor's hand, her voice steady despite the fear in her eyes. "We'll face it together. Whatever happens, we're not leaving without answers—and without your grandfather."

With renewed determination, the group pressed forward, the glowing path guiding them through the dense, shimmering woods. Each step brought them closer to the palace—and closer to the secrets that would change everything they thought they knew about Drakoria, the compass, and their own fates.

As they stepped inside the Drake Palace, a wave of warmth and calm washed over them. The palace shimmered with an otherworldly light, its walls etched with glowing patterns that seemed to shift and move, telling stories of a time long past. Brumble and Gruffle let out deep sighs of relief, their tense shoulders relaxing for the first time in what felt like ages.

"This place..." Gruffle said, his voice softer than usual. "It feels alive. So pure."

"It's the heart of Drakoria's goodness," Brumble addd. "No hatred, no evil can survive here. It's... home."

Victor and Clara exchanged a glance, feeling a sense of safety they hadn't experienced since entering this strange world.

"We need to start looking," Victor said, his determination rekindled. "For my grandfather. For the obsidian compass. For anything that gives us answers."

The group split up, moving through the vast halls of the palace. Golden lights flickered like stars on the ceiling, illuminating the intricate carvings on the walls. Statues of ancient Drakorians and depictions of a majestic creature—Drake, the leader of kindness—lined the corridors.

Clara stopped to examine a carving of the obsidian compass, its shape eerily familiar yet majestic in this artistic form. "Victor," she called, "this compass... it's connected to everything. Look at how it's surrounded by symbols of different worlds."

Victor nodded but felt a pull deeper into the palace. "I'll be back. I... I need to check something," he muttered and walked away, his steps guided by an invisible force.

As Victor wandered, the air seemed to hum around him, leading him to a grand chamber. At its center was a glowing pool of water, and on its edge sat an old man, his back hunched but his presence strong. Victor froze, his breath catching in his throat.

"Grandpa?" Victor whispered, his voice trembling.

The man turned slowly, his eyes wide with disbelief. "Victor?" His voice cracked, and tears welled up in his eyes. "Is it really you, my boy?"

Victor ran forward, dropping to his knees beside the man. "It's me, Grandpa. It's really me."

Max Morris Halloway pulled Victor into a tight embrace, his tears streaming freely. "I never thought... I never dreamed I'd see you again."

Victor held onto him, his own emotions overwhelming him. "I thought you were gone. We all did. But you're here. You're alive!"

The commotion drew Clara, Gruffle, and Brumble to the chamber. They stood in stunned silence as they watched the heartfelt reunion.

Clara wiped away tears as she knelt beside them. "You're Victor's grandfather. We've been looking for you."

Gruffle and Brumble stepped forward, their usual guarded demeanor replaced with joy. They embraced Max, their voices filled with relief. "You made it, old friend. You survived."

Max smiled, though his expression held deep sorrow. "I survived, but at a great cost." He looked at the group, his face serious now. "Sit. There's much to tell."

As they gathered around him, Max began to recount his journey. "When I first arrived here, I was like you—confused, scared, and desperate for answers. The obsidian compass brought me to Drakoria, and I learned of its power to connect worlds. But it also opened the door for noxmire and his forces to spread their evil."

He paused, his gaze distant. "I tried to fight back, to protect this world and find a way home. But the compass is not just a tool—it's a weapon, a key to controlling everything. Noxmire knew this and hunted me relentlessly. I escaped here, to the Drake Palace, the only place he couldn't reach."

Max's voice grew heavy with emotion. "But the palace is a prison as much as it is a sanctuary. I couldn't leave. I've been trapped here, waiting, hoping that someone—someone like you—would come."

Victor clenched his fists. "We're here now, Grandpa. We'll finish what you started. We'll stop noxmire and find a way to end this."

Max looked at him with a mixture of pride and fear. "It won't be easy, Victor. The obsidian compass is the key, but it's also the greatest danger. If noxmire gets his hands on it, no world will be safe."

Gruffle nodded solemnly. "Then we must act quickly. We have the blood to solve the riddles, the strength to fight, and the heart to stand against evil."

Max placed a hand on Victor's shoulder. "You are braver than I ever was, my boy. But remember, this fight will demand everything from you—all of you."

As the group sat in the glowing chamber, the weight of their mission settled over them. The stakes had never been higher, but together, they felt a spark of hope—a chance to end the cycle of destruction and bring light back to Drakoria and beyond.

Victor stood up abruptly, his expression stern and serious. "Grandpa," he said, stepping back. "We'll be right back. Stay here for a moment."

Max looked confused but nodded, sitting back down as Victor hurriedly motioned for Clara, Gruffle, and Brumble to follow him out of the chamber. Once they were in a quiet corner of the palace, away from Max's sight and earshot, Victor turned to the group with a heavy heart.

"That man..." Victor started, his voice trembling, "is not my grandfather."

Everyone froze, their faces a mix of shock and confusion. Clara was the first to break the silence. "What are you saying, Victor? You hugged him. You were crying. How can he not be your grandfather?"

Victor ran his hands through his hair, trying to steady himself. "He looks like him, talks like him, even knows things only my grandpa would know. But there's one thing that gave him away."

"What thing?" Gruffle asked, his claws twitching nervously.

Victor swallowed hard. "Until my grandpa disappeared, my name wasn't Victor. It was Smith. My parents changed my name after he vanished—something about wanting to leave the past behind. He only ever knew me as Smith. He wouldn't have called me Victor."

The realization hit the group like a thunderbolt. Clara's eyes widened. "Oh my god... then who is he?"

Brumble growled under his breath. "If he isn't your grandfather, then he's someone who wants us to believe he is. Someone with a reason to fool us."

Gruffle paced nervously. "We need to go back in there and figure out who he really is. If he's a spy for noxmire..."

Victor nodded, determination replacing his earlier hesitation. "We'll confront him, but carefully. If he's dangerous, we can't let him know we're onto him just yet."

Clara grabbed Victor's arm. "What if he's working with noxmire? What if this is all a trap?"

Victor's face hardened. "Then we'll deal with him, whatever it takes."

The group returned to the chamber, their expressions carefully neutral. Max—or whoever he was—looked up at them with a warm smile. "You're back. Did you discuss something important?"

Victor stepped forward, his heart pounding but his voice steady. "Yes, we did. And now I need to ask you something."

"Of course," Max said, his smile unwavering. "What is it?"

Victor stared into his eyes, searching for any hint of deception. "What was my name before my parents changed it?"

The question caught Max off guard. His smile faltered for just a second, but it was enough. "Your name?" he repeated, stalling. "It was... Victor, of course."

Victor's stomach sank, and he clenched his fists. "Wrong answer."

Max's expression darkened, his warm demeanor replaced by something cold and menacing. "Ah," he said, his voice dripping with mockery. "I see you're smarter than you look, boy."

Clara gasped, stepping back, while Gruffle and Brumble immediately positioned themselves defensively in front of Victor. "Who are you?" Gruffle growled, flames beginning to flicker in his palms.

The man who had been posing as Max stood up, his posture now radiating power and malice. His voice deepened, echoing unnaturally in the chamber. "I am someone who has watched you fools stumble through this world like lost children. And now, you've walked right into my hands."

Victor's blood ran cold. "You're... you're working with noxmire, aren't you?"

The imposter laughed, a chilling, hollow sound that reverberated through the chamber. "Working with noxmire? Oh, dear boy, I am noxmire's shadow. His eyes, his ears, his reach into places he cannot go himself."

Clara clutched Victor's arm, her voice trembling. "Victor, what do we do?"

Brumble stepped forward, his voice steady and commanding. "We fight."

Before anyone could react, the imposter lunged forward, his form shifting and twisting into a monstrous figure—dark, smoky tendrils swirling around him like a storm. The chamber seemed to shake as the air grew heavy with his power.

"Run!" Gruffle shouted, unleashing a burst of fire from his palms, forcing the creature to step back. "Get out of here! Now!"

Victor hesitated, torn between staying to fight and protecting Clara. "We can't just leave you!"

Brumble pushed him toward the exit. "Go! We'll hold him off. Find the real Max and the obsidian compass. It's the only way to stop noxmire!"

Reluctantly, Victor grabbed Clara's hand, and the two of them ran, their hearts pounding as the sounds of battle echoed behind them. The palace, once a sanctuary, now felt like a labyrinth of danger and betrayal. But Victor knew one thing for certain—this fight was far from over.

As Victor sprinted toward the sound of Gruffle's scream, Clara hesitated, fear gripping her heart. She glanced around, unsure whether to follow Victor or stay put. Her legs trembled, and her mind raced with panic. Suddenly, she spotted a dimly lit doorway and dashed into it, desperate for some sense of safety.

Inside, she found herself in what appeared to be a kitchen. It was unlike anything she'd ever seen—glowing utensils, bubbling cauldrons, and shelves lined with jars of luminous powders and liquids. As her eyes scanned the room, a handwritten recipe on a parchment caught her attention. The title read: Carpathian Matcha – The Ancient Brew.

Clara's heart skipped a beat. She remembered how much she loved drinking matcha, and something about the name "Carpathian" felt oddly significant. Could this brew have a connection to their journey? She decided to trust her instincts.

On the counter, a steaming pot of the glowing green matcha stood ready, along with empty jars nearby. Clara quickly filled two jars with the brew, sealing them tightly. She tucked them under her arm, unsure why she felt the need to carry them but certain they would come in handy.

Suddenly, a blood-curdling scream echoed through the palace, snapping Clara out of her thoughts. It came from above her, followed by loud crashes and roaring. Her pulse quickened. She had no idea what was happening but knew she had to act fast.

Clutching the jars, Clara ran toward the sound. Her feet carried her up a spiral staircase, and as she neared the source, she saw Victor struggling to fend off the monstrous fake Max. Gruffle lay unconscious nearby, his body motionless, while Brumble fought valiantly but seemed to be losing strength.

The fake Max roared, his dark, smoky form pulsating with rage. His fiery eyes locked onto Clara as she entered the scene. "You meddlesome humans!" he bellowed. "You will all perish here!"

Victor turned, relief washing over his face when he saw Clara. "Clara! Get back! It's too dangerous!"

But Clara wasn't listening. Her instincts kicked in, and she uncapped the jars. With a determined cry, she ran forward and hurled the contents of both jars directly onto the fake Max.

The glowing matcha splashed across his smoky form, sizzling like acid on contact. The creature let out an unearthly scream, writhing in pain as his form began to melt and dissolve. The room trembled as the dark energy surrounding him dissipated, leaving behind a charred, crumbling shell.

Victor stared in astonishment as Clara stood there, panting, clutching the empty jars. "Clara... what just happened?"

She looked at him, her face pale but resolute. "I don't know. I saw the matcha in the kitchen, and something told me it was important. I just... acted."

Brumble, injured but conscious, managed a weak chuckle. "The Carpathian Matcha," he said, his voice raspy. "It's a sacred brew... used to purify dark energy. Only the purest of hearts can wield it like that."

Victor rushed to Clara, pulling her into a tight hug. "You saved us. I don't know how, but you did."

Clara smiled faintly, her eyes glistening with tears. "I just couldn't let anything happen to you... or any of us."

Gruffle groaned from the floor, slowly sitting up. "What... what happened?"

Brumble helped him up, nodding toward Clara. "Our little human hero happened."

Victor turned to the group, determination burning in his eyes. "We have to keep going. If the matcha worked on that creature, maybe we're closer to finding the real Max—and the compass."

Clara nodded, gripping Victor's hand tightly. "Let's finish this together."

With renewed courage, they pressed on, leaving behind the remnants of the false Max and stepping closer to uncovering the truth about Drakoria—and Victor's destiny.

Victor and Clara were walking together through the glowing halls of the Drake Palace. The palace was huge, with walls that seemed alive, glowing softly like they were breathing. As they walked, Clara asked, "Victor, do you think we'll ever get back home?"

Victor looked at her and smiled faintly. "I don't know, Clara. But if we do, we'll have one crazy story to tell."

Clara laughed softly, but her laughter echoed strangely in the palace. It made her stop and look around. "This place is too quiet. It feels like it's watching us."

Victor shrugged, trying to hide his nervousness. "It's just a palace. It's old, magical, maybe. But it's just walls and rooms."

But deep inside, Victor also felt uneasy. The air felt heavy, and the glowing lights on the walls seemed dimmer than before.

Meanwhile, Gruffle and Brumble were walking in another part of the palace. Gruffle was laughing. "Brumble, remember when you got stuck in the glowing tree trunk because you thought you'd find a treasure inside?"

Brumble chuckled, shaking his head. "And you laughed so hard that you didn't notice the fireflies lighting your tail on fire."

They both laughed, but their laughter faded as they noticed something strange. The glow of the palace was flickering, and the air felt colder. Gruffle stopped laughing and said, "Something's wrong."

Victor and Clara kept walking, talking about their memories from Earth. Clara said, "You know, I used to dream about magical places like this. But now that we're here, it feels more like a nightmare."

Victor nodded. "I get it. This place is amazing but terrifying. It's like it wants us to stay but also wants us gone."

They turned a corner, and suddenly, Victor stopped. He looked around and frowned. "Wait... where are Gruffle and Brumble?"

Clara looked back and gasped. The glowing path they had been following was gone. The hallway behind them had turned into a solid wall. "Victor, what's happening?"

Victor tried to stay calm. "Maybe it's the palace. Maybe it's trying to confuse us."

Clara held his arm tightly. "We have to find them. I don't like this place anymore."

They turned another corner, hoping to find their way back, but the corridors seemed to change. Every turn looked the same, and soon, they were completely lost.

The air grew colder, and a strange whispering sound began to fill the hallway. Clara froze. "Victor... do you hear that?"

Victor nodded, his heart pounding. "Stay close to me. Don't let go of my hand."

The whispers grew louder, and they weren't just sounds anymore. They were words.

"Leave... outsiders... unworthy..."

Clara's eyes widened. "Victor, who's saying that?"

Victor shook his head. "I don't know. But we need to keep moving."

As they walked, the whispers turned into faint laughter. It was eerie, like someone was watching them and enjoying their fear.

Clara looked around, her voice trembling. "Victor, I think the palace is alive. It's playing with us."

Victor didn't answer. He just kept walking, his grip on Clara's hand tightening. He didn't want to admit it, but he felt the same.

Somewhere else in the palace, Gruffle and Brumble were shouting Victor and Clara's names, their voices echoing through the endless halls. But the palace seemed to twist and turn, keeping everyone apart.

Victor and Clara reached a dead end. The glowing wall in front of them had strange symbols carved into it. Victor touched the wall, hoping for some clue, but it was cold and unyielding.

"We're trapped," Clara whispered, her voice breaking.

"No," Victor said firmly. "We're not. We'll find a way out. We have to."

But deep inside, Victor wasn't sure anymore. The palace felt like a maze with no exit, and the whispers were getting louder.

"Turn back... or be lost forever..."

Victor looked at Clara and said, "Whatever happens, we stick together. Okay?"

Clara nodded, though tears filled her eyes. "Okay."

With no other choice, they turned back, hoping to find Gruffle and Brumble or some way to escape the palace's twisted corridors. But every step felt heavier, and the feeling of being watched never left them.

In the endless maze of the Drake Palace, the mystery grew darker, and the danger felt closer than ever.

Victor's mind was racing. He turned to Clara and whispered, "Clara, don't call me Victor anymore. Call me Smith."

Clara frowned, confused. "Why?"

Victor explained, "If my real grandpa is somewhere in this palace, he knows me as Smith. If he hears that name, he'll know I'm here. And it might also confuse whoever or whatever is watching us."

Clara nodded, understanding the plan. She took a deep breath and said loudly, "Smith, where do we go now?"

As soon as she said "Smith," the eerie whispers that surrounded them faded into silence. Victor and Clara looked at each other, relieved but cautious. Suddenly, a glowing path appeared before them, leading into the deeper parts of the palace.

Victor called out softly, "Gruffle! Brumble! Come quickly! We found something."

Gruffle and Brumble came running from a nearby hallway, their faces filled with worry. "What's happening?" Gruffle asked.

Victor pointed to the glowing path. "We're being guided somewhere. We need to follow it."

The four of them started walking down the glowing path, which twisted and turned through the palace. The air grew heavier, and the glow on the walls flickered like candles in the wind. After what felt like hours, they arrived at an ancient chamber.

The chamber was massive, with high ceilings and walls covered in intricate carvings. At the center of the room was an old stone pedestal, and on it lay a weathered, craved rock. The rock had glowing symbols etched into it, and beneath it was a riddle written in a language Victor didn't understand.

"What is this place?" Clara asked, her voice trembling.

Gruffle examined the carvings closely. "This is a sacred chamber. It's where the guardians of the palace used to leave clues and tests for those who dared enter. The riddle... it's a test. We must solve it to move forward."

Brumble squinted at the glowing text. "The riddle says we have to place something on this pedestal. But what?"

Victor stared at the riddle, trying to make sense of it. The symbols were strange, but Gruffle began to translate:
"The treasure of the heart,
The essence of the soul,
In its absence, none can be whole."

Clara whispered, "What does it mean? What treasure is it talking about?"

Victor thought for a moment. "It's something important. Something we can't live without."

Gruffle nodded. "But what is it? A memory? A feeling? Or something we carry with us?"

Brumble looked around the chamber. "It must be something that represents love or life. That's what this palace stands for."

Victor reached into his pocket and pulled out the pendant Clara had given him long ago. "Maybe it's this. It's a piece of my heart, something I care about deeply."

Clara smiled faintly. "You're really going to use that?"

Victor nodded. "If it helps us find my grandpa and the compass, it's worth it."

He placed the pendant on the pedestal, but nothing happened. The glow on the rock flickered, and the riddle remained unsolved.

"It's not enough," Gruffle said. "The riddle wants more."

Clara suddenly remembered the jars of matcha she had taken earlier. She pulled one out of her bag. "Maybe it's this! It's from Carpathian recipes, something tied to life and energy."

She poured a small amount of the matcha onto the pedestal. The symbols on the rock glowed brighter for a moment, but then dimmed again.

"It's close," Brumble said. "We're missing one piece."

Victor looked at the glowing text again. "The essence of the soul... maybe it's something only we can give."

Gruffle's eyes widened. "Blood. It's asking for blood. The palace is testing your courage and sacrifice."

Victor hesitated, then nodded. He took Clara's pendant and scratched his palm, letting a drop of blood fall onto the pedestal.

As soon as the blood touched the rock, the entire chamber lit up. The carvings on the walls glowed with a golden light, and the pedestal began to hum with energy. The riddle faded, and the stone pedestal cracked open, revealing a hidden compartment.

Inside was a small, glowing orb with a map etched into its surface. Gruffle picked it up carefully. "This is it. This will lead us to your grandfather and the compass."

Victor, Clara, Gruffle, and Brumble stared at the orb, their hearts pounding. The path ahead was still unknown, but they knew they were one step closer to uncovering the truth.

Gruffle stepped forward cautiously, his eyes locked on the glowing orb resting inside the cracked pedestal. "This must be it," he whispered, reaching out with his hand to take the map.

The moment his fingers touched the orb, a sharp jolt of energy surged through him. His hand flickered like a shadow, and he pulled back, groaning in pain.

Suddenly, a low, menacing whisper filled the chamber, echoing from every corner:
"You are in the domain of Max Morris Halloway. How dare you touch what is not yours?"

Everyone froze. Gruffle and Brumble looked around, their faces pale with fear. Clara clutched Victor's arm tightly, her breathing quick and shallow.

Victor, however, felt a strange familiarity in the voice. Taking a deep breath, he stepped forward and called out, "Grandpa! It's me, Smith!"

The whisper stopped abruptly, and the chamber fell silent. For a moment, nothing happened, and then the orb began to glow brighter, filling the room with a warm, golden light.

From the shadows, a figure emerged, slowly taking shape. It was an older man, with a kind face and weary eyes. His clothes were worn, and his hair was streaked with silver. Victor's heart raced as the figure stepped closer.

The man looked at Victor, his eyes narrowing as if trying to remember. Then, he whispered, "Smith... is it really you?"

Victor nodded, tears welling up in his eyes. "Yes, Grandpa. It's me. I've been searching for you."

The man's expression softened, and his lips trembled. "I never thought I'd see you again," he said, his voice cracking. He stepped forward and embraced Victor tightly.

Clara, Gruffle, and Brumble watched the emotional reunion in silence, their own eyes glistening with tears.

After a long moment, Max pulled back and looked at Victor. "How did you find me? And why are you here?"

Victor took a deep breath and explained everything—the Carpathian compass, the portal, the mysterious journey through Drakoria, and the riddle they had just solved. Max listened intently, his face a mixture of amazement and concern.

When Victor finished, Max looked at the glowing orb in the pedestal. "This map... it's the key to the obsidian compass. But getting to it won't be easy. Noxmire's forces will stop at nothing to prevent us from reaching it."

Gruffle stepped forward, his voice firm. "We've come this far, and we're not turning back now. Tell us what we need to do."

Max nodded, his expression determined. "We'll need to follow the map. It will guide us to the hidden chamber where the obsidian compass lies. But be warned—this palace is full of traps and illusions designed to test us. We must stay together and trust one another."

Clara tightened her grip on Victor's arm. "We've come too far to give up now. Let's do this."

Max looked at each of them, a glimmer of hope in his eyes. "Then let's move quickly. Every moment we waste brings Noxmire's forces closer to us. Together, we can finish what I started all those years ago."

With that, Max picked up the glowing orb. It hovered above his palm, projecting a shimmering map into the air. The path ahead was dangerous, but for the first time, Victor felt that they had a real chance to succeed.

And so, the group set off, their hearts united by a shared purpose, ready to face whatever challenges lay ahead.

Victor's steps quickened, his arms stretching out to embrace his grandfather. "Grandpa!" he called, his voice trembling with emotion. But just as he reached Max, something strange happened—his arms passed right through him.

Victor froze, stunned. He looked down at his hands, then back at Max, confusion clouding his face. "What... what's happening?"

Max gave a sorrowful smile, his eyes filled with a bittersweet sadness. "Victor, I'm not truly here. My body perished long ago. What you see before you is my soul, trapped in this cursed palace."

Victor's heart sank. "No... no, this can't be true! You're here, talking to me. How can you be... gone?"

Max placed a hand near Victor's shoulder, though it didn't truly touch him. "I died years ago, my boy. When the obsidian compass was activated by Noxmire, its dark magic tethered my soul to this place. I've been here ever since, guarding the secrets of Drakoria and hoping for someone brave enough to finish what I could not."

Clara gasped, her hand covering her mouth as tears welled up in her eyes. "Grandpa Max... this is so unfair!"

Gruffle and Brumble exchanged solemn glances. Gruffle muttered, "We always wondered why no Drakorian ever returned from this palace. Now we know—it traps not just bodies but spirits."

Victor's voice cracked as he asked, "Is there any way to set you free?"

Max's expression grew serious. "Yes, there is, but it won't be easy. My soul is bound to Noxmire's power. To free me, you must end his reign. Destroy him, and the curse he cast over this land—including me—will break."

Victor clenched his fists, determination replacing his despair. "Then we'll do it. We'll defeat Noxmire and end this nightmare, for you, for Drakoria, for everyone!"

Max's smile returned, faint but hopeful. "You have your mother's courage and your father's resolve, Victor. But be cautious. Noxmire is not just a foe of great power; he is cunning and ruthless. He will use your deepest fears against you."

Victor nodded. "We're ready for whatever comes our way."

Clara stepped forward, wiping her tears. "We're not leaving you behind, Grandpa Max. We'll do whatever it takes to set you free."

Gruffle and Brumble stood beside them, their faces stern. "We'll protect them, Max," Gruffle said. "You have our word."

Max gestured toward the glowing map in his hand. "Follow this. It will lead you to the chamber of the obsidian compass. But be wary—Noxmire's forces will be waiting. Trust each other, and trust yourselves. That is the only way you'll succeed."

As the group turned to leave, Victor paused, looking back at his grandfather. "We'll come back for you. I promise."

Max's voice was steady, yet tinged with emotion. "I believe in you, Victor. Now go. The fate of this world—and many others—rests in your hands."

With a heavy heart but unwavering determination, Victor joined the others as they ventured deeper into the palace, guided by the glowing map. The path ahead was fraught with danger, but their purpose was clear: to end Noxmire's tyranny and free Max's soul once and for all.

The group followed the glowing map cautiously, its faint shimmer guiding them through the winding corridors of Drake Palace. The path led them to a towering, ancient door etched with golden carvings and intricate symbols. Gruffle placed his hand on the door, his face solemn. "This is Dracia's door," he whispered.

Victor tilted his head. "Dracia? Who is she?"

Gruffle's voice grew heavy with emotion. "She was the queen of this land, the wife of Drake. She was the light of Drakoria, loved by every creature. But Noxmire, in his quest for ultimate power, sought to destroy Drake's strength. He captured Dracia and... sucked her soul. It's said her cries still echo in the void, and her presence was never felt again. It was a loss too painful to bear."

Clara shivered. "That's terrible. She was innocent."

Brumble nodded. "She was, and that's why this door is sacred. Few dare to pass through it, as her spirit is believed to guard it. But we must move forward."

They examined the symbols on the door and noticed a riddle inscribed on its surface:

"Only those who understand loss, seek truth, and hold courage may enter."

Victor frowned, reading the words aloud. "What does it mean?"

Clara thought for a moment. "Loss... truth... courage. Maybe we need to prove these things somehow."

Gruffle found three stone pedestals near the door, each marked with a word from the riddle. "It must be these," he said. "We need to place something that represents loss, truth, and courage."

Victor placed his pendant, gifted by Clara, on the "Loss" pedestal. Clara placed her notebook, filled with sketches of the world she longed to explore, on the "Truth" pedestal. Brumble pulled out a small, glowing dagger and set it on the "Courage" pedestal.

The door creaked open, revealing a dimly lit chamber. The air felt heavy, as though carrying the weight of countless untold stories. At the center of the room was a glowing box, precisely where the map indicated.

They approached it cautiously, unsure of what they would find. "This must be it," Victor said.

But Clara hesitated. "What's inside? Why does it feel… wrong?"

Brumble stepped forward, determination in his eyes. "There's only one way to know."

Without waiting for a reply, Brumble opened the box and stepped inside. The moment he did, a loud, bone-chilling scream erupted. The floor beneath them trembled violently, and suddenly, they felt as though they were falling through an endless void.

Victor yelled, reaching for Clara, who clung tightly to him. Gruffle roared, trying to stabilize himself, but the pull was too strong. The darkness around them was thick, suffocating, and the scream echoed louder and louder until it consumed everything.

And then—silence.

They landed abruptly on a cold, stone floor, gasping for breath. A dim red light illuminated the chamber they were now in. Gruffle looked around, his eyes wide with shock. "Where… are we?"

Victor stood, helping Clara to her feet. "This wasn't on the map. What just happened?"

In the center of the room was another glowing object—an orb, pulsing with a strange, dark energy. On the walls were carvings of Dracia, her face twisted in pain, surrounded by shadowy figures.

Clara shuddered. "I think... I think we're inside Dracia's sorrow. This is her pain, her prison."

Gruffle's voice trembled. "Then we need to be careful. If her soul still lingers here, she might not recognize us as allies. And if Noxmire's magic is in control..."

Before he could finish, a ghostly figure began to materialize in the room. It was Dracia, her once-beautiful form now distorted, her eyes glowing with an eerie blue light. She spoke, her voice echoing with anguish:

"Who dares disturb my eternal slumber? Leave, or face the wrath of the lost queen!"

The group froze, unsure of how to respond. Victor stepped forward, his voice shaking but firm. "We're not here to harm you. We're here to stop Noxmire and free this land. Please... we need your help!"

Dracia's figure flickered, her expression torn between rage and sorrow. "You speak of freedom, yet you awaken the pain I've buried. Why should I trust you?"

Victor exchanged a glance with Clara, then turned back to Dracia. "Because we've suffered loss too. We've seen what Noxmire has done. And we won't stop until we end his reign. Please... we need to know how to defeat him."

Dracia stared at them, her form wavering. Finally, she spoke: "If you seek to end Noxmire, you must face the darkness within yourselves. Only then will you find the strength to destroy him. But beware—his power is vast, and his hatred knows no bounds."

With those words, she extended her hand, and the orb in the center of the room began to glow brighter. "Take this," she said. "It holds the key to his downfall. But tread carefully. The path ahead is fraught with peril."

As the orb floated toward them, Victor reached out and took it, feeling its warmth and weight. "Thank you," he said.

Dracia's figure began to fade, her voice echoing softly as she disappeared. "Go now... and do what I could not. Save Drakoria."

The group stood in silence, the gravity of their mission sinking in. With the orb in hand, they turned to leave the chamber, determined to face whatever lay ahead.

The group stepped out of Dracia's chamber, following the map's glowing trail. It led them through a narrow, winding path that soon opened into a dense, eerie forest. The air was thick with mist, and the trees looked twisted, their branches curling like claws. Strange sounds echoed—low growls, whispers, and rustling leaves.

Clara held Victor's hand tightly. "This place feels alive, Victor. Like it's watching us."

Gruffle sniffed the air, his expression tense. "We are in the Forest of Whispers. This is no ordinary forest. It's said that those who enter hear their deepest fears and desires. Stay close, and don't listen to anything you hear."

Brumble nodded in agreement. "And keep moving. The forest has a way of trapping you if you stop for too long."

As they ventured deeper, the whispers grew louder. Clara suddenly froze, her eyes wide. "Victor, did you hear that? It sounded like my mother calling me."

Victor gently shook her. "Clara, it's not real. Remember what Gruffle said—it's trying to trick us."

Gruffle growled. "Don't listen to the voices. Focus on the path."

But just as he said that, a rustling sound came from behind them. They turned to see shadowy figures emerging from the mist—Noxmire's soldiers.

"They've found us!" Brumble yelled, drawing his glowing dagger.

The soldiers were terrifying—humanoid but covered in black armor that seemed to pulse like a heartbeat. Their eyes glowed red, and they moved with unnatural speed.

Gruffle let out a fierce roar, breathing fire at the first wave of soldiers. Brumble slashed at another, his movements quick and precise. Victor and Clara stayed behind them, trying to dodge the attacks.

One soldier lunged at Victor, but he grabbed a broken branch from the ground and swung it with all his strength. The soldier staggered, giving Gruffle a chance to incinerate it.

Clara threw a stone at another soldier, but it had no effect. "Victor, what do we do? They're too strong!"

Victor scanned the area and noticed a narrow gap between two massive trees. "We need to run! Through there!"

The group sprinted through the gap, the soldiers chasing close behind. The forest seemed to come alive, with vines and roots tangling the soldiers' feet, slowing them down.

After running for what felt like hours, they burst out of the forest and came to an abrupt stop. Before them was a massive river of fire, its flames roaring and crackling like a living beast.

The heat was intense, making it hard to breathe. In the center of the river, suspended on a pedestal of black stone, was a glass box glowing faintly. Inside, something dark and shimmering caught their eye—it looked like the obsidian compass.

Victor pointed. "That's it! It has to be the compass!"

Gruffle stepped forward but stopped abruptly. "Wait. This isn't just a river of fire. It's alive. Look."

The flames began to rise, forming shapes—fiery creatures with glowing eyes and sharp claws. They looked like they were guarding the box.

Clara whispered, "How are we supposed to get across? That's impossible!"

Brumble examined the area and noticed a series of stones sticking out of the fire, forming a jagged path to the pedestal. "There's a way, but it's dangerous. Those stones won't hold for long, and the fire guardians will attack."

Victor looked determined. "We have to try. Clara, stay here with Gruffle. Brumble and I will go."

Clara protested, "No, I'm coming too! We're in this together."

Gruffle sighed. "Fine. But stay behind me. I'll clear the way."

The group carefully stepped onto the first stone, feeling the intense heat beneath their feet. Gruffle led the way, using his fire-breath to push back the fiery creatures that lunged at them.

As they moved from stone to stone, the path began to crumble behind them. Clara nearly slipped, but Victor caught her arm just in time.

"Careful!" he said, pulling her up.

They finally reached the pedestal, but as Victor reached for the glass box, a loud roar shook the air. A massive fiery serpent emerged from the river, its eyes glowing like molten lava.

"It's guarding the compass!" Brumble shouted.

The serpent lashed out, its fiery tail whipping toward them. Gruffle blocked it with a wall of flames, but the force sent him stumbling backward.

Victor yelled, "We need to distract it!"

Clara grabbed a handful of stones from her bag and threw them at the serpent's head. It hissed angrily and turned toward her.

"Now, Victor!" she screamed.

Victor quickly grabbed the glass box, but it wouldn't budge. "It's stuck!" he shouted.

Brumble stepped forward, placing his glowing dagger against the pedestal. "This should do it!" With a sharp twist, the pedestal cracked, and the box came free.

The serpent roared in fury, its flames growing larger and hotter. The group turned and ran back across the crumbling stones, the serpent chasing them.

As they reached the edge of the river, Gruffle turned and unleashed his strongest fire-breath yet, creating a massive explosion that sent the serpent retreating into the flames.

They collapsed on the ground, panting and sweating. Victor held the glass box tightly. "We did it. We got the compass."

Clara looked at the glowing box, her face filled with determination. "One step closer to stopping Noxmire."

Gruffle nodded. "But the battle is far from over. The hardest part is yet to come."

The group stood, their resolve stronger than ever, and prepared to follow the map to their next destination.

Victor held the glass box tightly, staring at the supposed obsidian compass inside. Clara leaned closer, her voice trembling. "Finally, we have it... but something feels off, Victor. It's too easy."

Gruffle and Brumble exchanged worried glances. Brumble added, "True treasures of power are never unguarded like this. Be cautious."

Victor looked around and noticed an old, half-melted candle on a nearby ledge. "Maybe this has something to do with it," he said, lighting it.

As soon as the flame flickered, the room darkened, and the compass inside the box began to glow ominously. Suddenly, the glow expanded, forming a swirling portal.

"Wait, what's happening?" Clara screamed, clutching Victor's arm tightly.

The portal grew larger, spinning faster, and before they could react, it pulled all four of them into its vortex. They screamed as the force dragged them through, spiraling into nothingness.

When they landed, the group found themselves in a pitch-black room. The air was heavy and suffocating, filled with the weight of unseen evil. The ground beneath them was cold and damp, and a sinister energy surrounded them, pressing against their chests like a vice.

Victor gasped for breath, struggling to stand. "Where are we? What is this place?"

Clara clung to him, her voice trembling. "I don't know, but it feels... wrong. So, so wrong."

Gruffle and Brumble growled lowly, their eyes scanning the darkness. "This is not Drakoria," Gruffle said. "This is a cursed space... a prison for spirits. We shouldn't be here!"

Suddenly, whispers began echoing all around them, voices filled with anger, sorrow, and malice. The room seemed alive, pulsating with dark energy.

"Humans... you dare to enter?" a deep, guttural voice boomed, shaking the room.

Clara screamed, clutching her ears. The voices grew louder, turning into piercing shrieks. Victor fell to his knees, clutching his chest as an unbearable pressure crushed him. Gruffle and Brumble roared in pain, their bodies trembling under the oppressive energy.

"I can't breathe," Clara choked, tears streaming down her face.

Victor forced himself to his feet, his hands trembling. "We can't stay here! There must be a way out!"

The voice boomed again, mocking them. "There is no escape. This is the shadow realm... the grave of those who dared defy Noxmire."

The room began to shift and change, the darkness morphing into shadowy figures. These figures surrounded them, their hollow eyes glowing faintly. They reached out with bony, claw-like hands, their touch icy and painful.

Brumble yelled, "Stay together! Don't let them separate us!"

Victor gritted his teeth and grabbed Clara's hand. "We have to fight it! We have to push through!"

Gruffle roared, unleashing a stream of fire, but the flames were quickly absorbed by the darkness. "My powers... they're useless here!"

The shadows closed in, their whispers turning into bone-chilling screams. Clara cried out, "What do they want from us?"

Victor's eyes darted around, searching for anything that might help. Then he remembered the glowing compass in the box. He fumbled with the latch and opened the glass casing. The compass shimmered faintly, pulsating like a heartbeat.

"Maybe this is the key!" Victor shouted, holding it up.

The shadows recoiled slightly, their movements hesitant. But the dark voice roared again. "You think the compass will save you? Foolish mortal!"

The compass's glow began to dim, and Victor's heart sank. Clara gripped his arm. "Don't give up! There has to be a way to use it!"

Brumble's eyes lit up with realization. "The compass is connected to the portal! It's a bridge! Focus on where you want to go, Victor!"

Victor closed his eyes, his hands trembling as he gripped the compass tightly. He concentrated, thinking of the palace, the light, and freedom from the shadows.

The compass began to glow brighter, its light piercing through the darkness. The shadows shrieked in pain, retreating as the light grew stronger.

"Hold on!" Victor yelled.

A portal began to form, swirling with light and color. The group huddled together, and Gruffle shouted, "Jump!"

They leapt into the portal just as the shadows lunged at them, their icy claws narrowly missing.

They tumbled out onto solid ground, gasping for air. The oppressive energy was gone, replaced by a calm, glowing light. They looked around to find themselves back in the palace, standing before a grand chamber bathed in golden light.

Victor held the compass tightly, his knuckles white. "That wasn't the real compass... it was a trap."

Brumble nodded, his face grim. "And now we know how dangerous Noxmire's tricks can be."

Clara shivered, wiping her tears. "We need to find the real one... and fast."

Gruffle growled, his eyes narrowing. "The battle has only just begun."

They stood together, their resolve stronger than ever, determined to uncover the truth and end Noxmire's reign of terror.

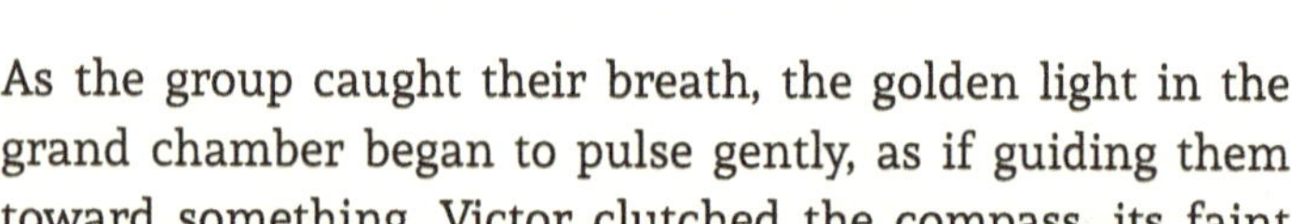

As the group caught their breath, the golden light in the grand chamber began to pulse gently, as if guiding them toward something. Victor clutched the compass, its faint glow reassuring him, but questions still filled his mind.

Clara broke the silence. "If that wasn't the real compass, then where is it? How much more do we have to go through?"

Gruffle sniffed the air, his expression hardening. "This chamber holds secrets, but it's not safe. We need to move quickly before Noxmire's forces catch up."

Brumble pointed toward the far end of the chamber, where an enormous door stood. It was carved with intricate symbols and glowing faintly. "That door... it's hiding something important. The energy is different there."

Victor nodded. "Then let's check it out."

As they approached the door, it seemed to hum softly, vibrating under their gaze. Clara reached out to touch it, but Gruffle stopped her. "Wait! These doors are often protected by riddles or traps. Let me examine it first."

Gruffle studied the symbols closely, running his claws over the carvings. He muttered, "These marks... they're ancient Drakonian, written in layers of riddles."

Victor stepped closer, his curiosity piqued. "Can you read it?"

Gruffle sighed. "Not all of it. But this part says, 'Only the brave with hearts pure and true may unlock what lies beyond.'"

Clara frowned. "What does that mean? Do we have to prove something?"

Brumble tilted his head thoughtfully. "It's likely a test. These doors often measure your spirit and intentions. If anyone here has doubts, they won't let us pass."

Victor exchanged a glance with Clara. "We have no choice but to try."

Gruffle nodded and placed his hand firmly on the door. The symbols flared with light, and the room began to shift. The floor beneath them rumbled, and the door creaked open slowly, revealing a swirling mist beyond.

"Stay close," Brumble warned. "We don't know what's on the other side."

The group stepped into the mist, their footsteps echoing in the silence. The air felt dense and electric, sending shivers down their spines. Suddenly, the mist began to clear, and they found themselves standing in a vast, circular arena.

In the center of the arena stood a pedestal, and on it rested a gleaming object. It was small, black, and faintly glowing—the real obsidian compass.

Victor's heart raced. "We found it!"

But before they could take a step forward, a deep, bone-chilling laugh echoed around them. The arena darkened, and shadows began to swirl in the air.

"Well, well... brave little intruders," a voice boomed. It was deep and filled with malice, vibrating through their very bones.

Clara clung to Victor's arm. "Is that... Noxmire?"

Gruffle growled, stepping in front of the group protectively. "Show yourself, coward!"

The shadows gathered into a towering figure. It had glowing red eyes, sharp claws, and an aura of pure hatred. It was Noxmire himself, his presence overwhelming.

"You've come far," Noxmire sneered, his voice dripping with mockery. "But you will not take what is mine."

Victor stood firm, gripping the compass tightly. "This compass doesn't belong to you. It's the key to ending your tyranny!"

Noxmire let out a dark chuckle. "Foolish human. You think you can defeat me? You're nothing but dust under my feet."

Suddenly, the arena floor began to crack, and shadowy creatures emerged, their glowing eyes locked onto the group.

Brumble roared, "Get ready! This is it!"

Gruffle unleashed a stream of fire, keeping the creatures at bay. Clara grabbed Victor's hand, her voice trembling but firm. "We have to reach the compass, no matter what."

Victor nodded. "Stick together. Don't let them separate us!"

The battle began. Shadows swarmed around them, their claws slashing through the air. Gruffle and Brumble fought fiercely, their combined strength pushing back the creatures. Clara and Victor weaved through the chaos, dodging attacks as they made their way toward the pedestal.

Noxmire watched from above, his laughter echoing. "You're wasting your time. None of you will leave here alive!"

Victor clenched his fists, determination burning in his eyes. "We're not giving up!"

As they neared the pedestal, the shadows grew denser, their attacks more relentless. Clara tripped and fell, a shadow closing in on her.

"Clara!" Victor shouted, slashing at the creature with a sharp fragment of stone he found. He pulled her to her feet. "We're almost there. Don't stop now!"

Finally, they reached the pedestal. The obsidian compass glowed brighter as Victor approached. He hesitated for a moment, his hand hovering over it.

"Victor, hurry!" Clara urged.

Victor grabbed the compass, and a blinding light erupted from it, pushing the shadows back. Noxmire roared in anger, his form flickering.

"This isn't over!" Noxmire bellowed, his voice fading as the light consumed the arena.

When the light dimmed, the group found themselves back in the palace, the compass glowing faintly in Victor's hands. They were battered and bruised, but alive.

Gruffle looked at Victor, pride in his eyes. "You did it. You got the compass."

Victor nodded, his grip tightening on the object. "But this is just the beginning. We have to use this to end Noxmire for good."

The group exchanged determined looks, ready for whatever came next. They had the compass, but the final battle was still ahead.

Victor, Clara, and Gruffle stood at the edge of the Holy Drake River, staring at the gleaming glass box. The water shimmered with a golden glow, and the air was filled with a hum, as if the river itself was alive and waiting.

"This must be the place," Gruffle said, his voice low.

Victor nodded and stepped forward cautiously, holding the obsidian compass tightly. He looked at Clara, who gave him an encouraging nod. Slowly, he placed the compass into the glass box.

The moment it touched the surface, the box began to glow brightly. The river surged with energy, and the glass opened like a blooming lotus. Six spoon-like structures emerged, each glowing faintly and vibrating with a unique hum.

"What... what is this?" Clara whispered, stepping closer.

Gruffle narrowed his eyes, studying the spoons. "It's a test. The spoons are asking for something, but what?"

Victor noticed faint inscriptions on each spoon. The words glowed faintly, but they were in an ancient script. "Gruffle, can you read this?"

Gruffle leaned in, squinting at the inscriptions. After a moment, he said, "Each spoon is asking for an offering—something that symbolizes the essence of the Holy Drake River. Only the right offerings will unlock the box completely."

Clara frowned. "Essence? What kind of offerings?"

Gruffle pointed to the first spoon. "This one says, 'The tears of the brave.' It needs something that represents courage."

Victor looked at Clara. "Do you think...?"

Clara's eyes widened. "The compass. It represents the courage of your grandfather and us coming here. Should we use it?"

Gruffle shook his head. "No. The compass is the key to defeating Noxmire. We need something else."

Victor thought for a moment, then pulled out a small pendant from his pocket. It was a gift from his parents, a reminder of his family's love and strength. "Maybe this will work."

He placed the pendant on the first spoon. The spoon glowed brightly, and the hum grew louder.

"It worked!" Clara exclaimed.

Gruffle nodded. "One down, five to go."

He read the next spoon. "This one says, 'The breath of life.'"

Clara looked around, then spotted a golden flower growing near the riverbank. Its petals shimmered as if alive. She plucked it gently and placed it on the second spoon. The flower dissolved into light, and the spoon glowed.

Gruffle read the third inscription. "'The spark of wisdom.'"

Brumble's voice echoed from behind them. "Wisdom comes from experience, but also from sacrifice. Use something that holds meaning."

Victor reached into his bag and pulled out a small notebook. It was filled with sketches and notes from his grandfather's discoveries. "This has guided me so far. Maybe it's enough."

He placed the notebook on the third spoon. It too dissolved into light, and the spoon glowed.

The fourth spoon read, "'The heart of kindness.'"

Clara stepped forward, holding a bracelet made of tiny beads. "This was given to me by my little sister before I left home. It's filled with love and kindness."

She placed it on the spoon, and it glowed brightly.

Gruffle read the fifth spoon. "'The shadow of truth.'"

Victor frowned. "Shadow of truth? What does that mean?"

Gruffle thought for a moment, then said, "It means something that reveals but also hides—a duality."

Victor hesitated, then pulled out an old compass that his grandfather had once used for navigation. "This has guided me, but it's also hidden secrets. Maybe it's enough."

He placed the compass on the spoon, and it dissolved into light.

Finally, they reached the sixth spoon. Gruffle read the inscription. "'The fire of hope.'"

Gruffle stepped forward. "I know what this needs."

He placed his hand over the spoon and blew a small stream of fire from his palm. The fire swirled into the spoon, which glowed brightly.

As all six spoons glowed in unison, the glass box began to tremble. The river surged with energy, and the box opened fully, revealing a crystal orb inside. The orb pulsed with a powerful light, filling the area with warmth.

Victor reached out to touch it, but Gruffle stopped him. "Careful. This orb is ancient and powerful. It could hold the key to defeating Noxmire, or it could be a trap."

Victor nodded and carefully picked up the orb. The moment he did, the river calmed, and the glowing spoons retreated into the box.

"This is it," Victor said softly. "The final piece to end this once and for all."

As they turned to leave, the ground shook violently. The sky above darkened, and a chilling laugh echoed through the air.

"You thought it would be that easy?" Noxmire's voice boomed. "Fools! The game has only just begun!"

Shadows began to rise from the river, swirling around them menacingly. Victor clutched the orb tightly, determination in his eyes.

"We won't let you win," he said firmly.

Gruffle, Clara, and Brumble stood by his side, ready to face whatever came next. Their journey was far from over, but their resolve had never been stronger.

Gruffle took some water from the Holy Drake River and threw it into the fire. The fire changed. Bright light covered everything. When the light was gone, they saw they were in a new place.

This place was so pretty! The ground had flowers in all colors—red, blue, yellow, and more. The sky was light blue, and there were soft white clouds. The air smelled sweet, like flowers. It felt warm and happy, like a big hug.

Clara spun around and said, "Wow! This is amazing!"

Victor touched a glowing flower and whispered, "It's like a dream."

Gruffle smiled. "This place feels so good. It's like home."

But Brumble looked serious. "This place is nice—too nice. What if it's a trick? Noxmire is smart. He makes traps that feel real."

Victor nodded. "You're right. We have to be careful. But we also need to rest. Let's sleep here tonight and leave when the sun comes up."

They agreed. They found a big tree with shiny silver leaves and sat under it. The air was so calm. It felt like the wind was singing.

Clara broke the silence. "Do you remember when we first got here? I was so scared. But now, I feel like we are close to something big, something important."

Victor smiled. "Yes. I didn't think this would happen, but it feels like everything in my life brought me here."

Gruffle laughed. "It's funny. Brumble and I lived in Drakoria our whole lives. But we never thought we'd meet humans—or go on an adventure like this."

Brumble laughed too. "Gruffle, remember when you ate that glowing fruit, and you hiccupped fire for three days?"

Everyone started laughing.

Clara laughed so much her eyes watered. "Gruffle, fire hiccups? I can't imagine that! It must have been so funny!"

They kept telling stories and making jokes. Victor talked about his grandpa and how much he missed him. Clara spoke about her little sister and how she missed her family. Gruffle and Brumble told silly stories about their childhood, running through forests and causing trouble.

They all felt happy and safe. For the first time in a long time, they weren't scared. They were just friends sitting together and laughing.

Later, they lay down under the tree. The stars in the sky twinkled. Everything was so quiet and calm. They fell asleep with smiles on their faces, feeling peaceful.

But far away, something was watching them. It was quiet and hidden in the dark. It waited. This happy place wasn't as safe as it seemed. Something bad was coming.

11

When the sun rose, its soft light filled the beautiful place. Clara was the first to wake up. She stretched her arms and looked around. Everything was quiet, too quiet.

She glanced at the spot where Gruffle had slept. It was empty.

"Gruffle?" Clara called softly. No answer.

She stood up and looked behind the big tree. Then she checked near the glowing flowers and the shiny river. Gruffle wasn't anywhere. Her heart started beating fast.

"Gruffle! Where are you?" she yelled, louder this time.

Her voice woke up Brumble and Victor. They sat up, rubbing their eyes.

"What's wrong, Clara?" Victor asked, worried.

"Gruffle is gone!" Clara said, her voice shaking. "I woke up, and he's not here. I looked everywhere!"

Brumble jumped to his feet. His face turned serious. "Gone? That's not good. Gruffle wouldn't leave without telling us. Something's wrong."

Victor stood beside Clara and held her hand. "We'll find him. Don't worry."

Brumble sniffed the air like he was tracking something. "I smell something... strange. It's not the same as this place. It smells like... smoke. Maybe fire."

Victor looked around. "Could Noxmire's shadows have reached us? What if this place wasn't as safe as we thought?"

Clara's eyes filled with tears. "We shouldn't have stayed here. What if something bad happened to Gruffle because of us?"

Brumble put his hand on her shoulder. "Don't blame yourself, Clara. We'll find him. Gruffle is strong. He wouldn't go down without a fight."

Victor nodded. "Let's split up and look. But don't go too far. Call out if you see anything strange."

They all started searching the area. Clara checked near the glowing flowers again, hoping Gruffle was hiding there. Brumble followed the smell of smoke, his face full of worry. Victor climbed a small hill to get a better view.

"Gruffle!" they all called out, their voices echoing.

Suddenly, Brumble yelled, "I found something!"

Victor and Clara ran toward him. Brumble was standing near a patch of crushed flowers. There were big claw marks on the ground, and the grass was burned.

"This is Gruffle's fire," Brumble said, pointing at the scorched ground. "He fought something here."

Victor knelt down and touched the marks. "But who or what did he fight? And where did they take him?"

Clara hugged herself tightly, shivering. "We have to find him. He's our friend. He's always protected us. Now it's our turn to protect him."

Brumble nodded. "If Gruffle is in trouble, we'll save him. No matter what."

Victor clenched his fists. "Let's follow these marks. They'll lead us to Gruffle—and whatever took him."

With heavy hearts but determined minds, they followed the trail, hoping they weren't too late.

They followed the footsteps, growing more anxious with every step. The hours felt like days as they wandered through the forest, only to realize they were walking in circles. The same shiny trees, the same glowing flowers, the same strange rock with a crack in the middle—they kept appearing, no matter how far they walked.

"This isn't normal," Victor muttered, frustrated.

"It's a loop," Brumble said firmly. "A magical maze designed to trap us. If we don't figure it out, we'll be stuck here forever."

Clara's voice trembled. "But how do we break it? There's nothing here!"

Victor clenched his fists. "There has to be a way. Every maze has a weak point. Something we're missing."

Brumble nodded, his sharp eyes scanning the surroundings. "We need to find the heart of this loop—the thing that's keeping us trapped."

They began searching every corner of the maze. Clara poked at the glowing flowers, Victor tapped the trees to see if they were hollow, and Brumble sniffed the air for any sign of magic. But nothing seemed out of place.

Just when they were losing hope, Clara noticed something odd. "Wait... this flower isn't glowing like the others."

Victor and Brumble rushed over. The flower she pointed to was dull, its petals a deep violet instead of the bright golden glow of the others.

Brumble frowned. "That's strange. It's different. It doesn't belong here."

Victor crouched down, inspecting the flower. As he touched it, the petals fell away, revealing a small, shimmering vial hidden beneath it. The vial contained a swirling liquid, black as night with specks of silver light dancing inside.

"What is this?" Clara whispered, her voice filled with awe.

Brumble's eyes widened. "A Memory Elixir. Rare and dangerous. It's said to hold the truth of whoever opens it. This could be the key."

Victor hesitated. "What do we do with it? Drink it?"

Brumble shook his head. "No, that's too risky. The riddle said something about offering what's true. Maybe the elixir needs to reveal something about us—something hidden."

Clara looked uneasy. "But what if it shows something we don't want to see?"

Victor took a deep breath. "We have no choice. We're running out of time, and Gruffle is counting on us."

Victor opened the vial. As soon as he did, the black liquid swirled into the air, forming shapes and images. The forest around them grew still, and the maze seemed to hum with energy.

The liquid shaped itself into a scene from Victor's past—a moment he had buried deep in his memory. It showed a young Victor, sitting alone in his room, holding a drawing of a compass. He was crying softly, saying, "Grandpa, I'll find you one day. I promise."

Clara gasped. "Victor... is that you?"

Victor nodded, his voice breaking. "It was right after Grandpa disappeared. I used to draw the compass over and over, thinking it would somehow bring him back."

The swirling liquid dissolved, and the ground beneath them trembled. A path opened before them, leading out of the loop.

Brumble smiled. "The maze needed something true—something from the heart. Your promise to your grandfather was enough to break it."

Victor held Clara's hand tightly. "Let's go. We're getting closer."

Together, they stepped onto the new path, their determination stronger than ever. The air felt lighter, and for the first time in hours, they felt hope. But deep down, they all knew—the real challenge was still ahead.

As they stepped out of the maze, a wave of relief washed over them. The endless loop, the glowing trees, the swirling confusion—it was all behind them now. They sat down to catch their breath, unsure of what lay ahead.

Victor sighed. "We made it out... but now what? We still don't know where to go next."

Clara nodded, looking around at the endless expanse of the mysterious forest. "We can't keep wandering aimlessly. There must be a sign or something to guide us."

Before anyone could speak further, they heard a rustling behind them. Victor and Clara jumped to their feet, ready for danger. Brumble raised his staff, prepared to defend.

Suddenly, Gruffle burst out from the trees, panting heavily. "Hey! There you are!"

Victor blinked in shock. "Gruffle? Where have you been? We've been searching everywhere for you!"

Clara crossed her arms, her face both relieved and annoyed. "You just disappeared without saying anything! We thought something terrible happened!"

Gruffle scratched the back of his head, avoiding their eyes. "Oh, um... I had to, uh... chase a glowing butterfly."

"A glowing butterfly?" Brumble raised an eyebrow, clearly unimpressed.

"Yes! It was... very important," Gruffle insisted, his voice nervous. "You see, in Drakoria, glowing butterflies are, uh, good luck charms! I thought if I caught one, it would help us!"

Victor groaned. "Gruffle, we were stuck in a maze for hours! And you were chasing butterflies?"

Gruffle raised his hands defensively. "Hey! I didn't mean to get lost! But look, I found my way back, didn't I?"

Clara sighed, shaking her head. "You're lucky we didn't run into something worse."

Brumble gave Gruffle a stern look. "Next time, don't wander off. This isn't a game. We're in dangerous territory."

Gruffle nodded quickly. "Right, right. No more butterfly chasing. I promise."

Victor couldn't help but laugh a little, despite his frustration. "Well, you're here now. Let's stick together this time."

As they regrouped, a soft glow appeared in the distance, drawing their attention. It wasn't like the maze or the glowing trees—it was steady, warm, and inviting, as if calling to them.

Clara pointed. "Maybe that's where we need to go next."

Gruffle squinted at the light and nodded. "That's not just any glow... that's Drake's Beacon! It's said to guide those who seek truth."

Brumble smiled faintly. "Then let's not waste any more time. If the beacon is shining for us, it means we're on the right path."

As they walked toward the glowing beacon, Gruffle suddenly stopped, his face serious. "Wait," he said, his voice unusually calm. "We need to change our plan."

Victor, Clara, and Brumble turned to him in confusion.

"What do you mean, change our plan?" Victor asked. "We're finally on the right path. The beacon—"

Gruffle interrupted, "The beacon is fine, but if we want to truly defeat Noxmire and free this world, we need to go somewhere else first. We need to go to Noxmire's Prison."

Everyone froze. Brumble's face turned pale. "Noxmire's Prison? Have you gone mad, Gruffle? That's the most dangerous place in all of Drakoria! No one who goes there ever comes out!"

Clara looked alarmed. "Why would we even think of going there? What could we possibly gain from such a place?"

Gruffle's eyes gleamed strangely as he spoke. "There's something there we need. Something Noxmire doesn't want anyone to find. A key. Without it, we can't stop him."

Victor frowned, his voice cautious. "Gruffle... how do you know this? You've been acting strange ever since you disappeared. What's going on?"

Gruffle avoided their eyes and muttered, "I just... I know, okay? Trust me on this. I wouldn't suggest it if it wasn't important."

Brumble crossed his arms, clearly unconvinced. "You're hiding something. Spill it, Gruffle. Why should we risk our lives walking into Noxmire's domain?"

Gruffle hesitated, his usually cheerful demeanor replaced by an unsettling seriousness. "Look, I can't explain everything right now. But the prison holds answers we need—about the compass, about your grandfather, Victor, and maybe even about how to end this once and for all. I feel it in my bones."

Victor exchanged a wary glance with Clara, who was biting her lip nervously. "If we do this," Victor said slowly, "we need to be prepared. Really prepared. This isn't just some maze or glowing forest. This is Noxmire's territory."

Clara nodded, gripping Victor's arm. "I don't like this, but if Gruffle's right... we can't ignore it."

Brumble sighed heavily. "Fine. If we're doing this, we need to stick together. No wandering off, no surprises." He shot a pointed look at Gruffle, who smiled sheepishly.

Gruffle nodded. "Understood. But trust me, this is the right path."

As they turned away from the beacon and toward the shadowy horizon, the air grew colder and heavier with every step. Gruffle led the way, his usual chatter replaced by a tense silence.

Victor couldn't shake the feeling that something wasn't right. "Gruffle," he asked quietly as they walked, "are you sure this is the only way?"

Gruffle didn't answer immediately. When he finally spoke, his voice was barely a whisper. "Sometimes, the darkest paths lead to the brightest light."

Gruffle was walking ahead of everyone, leading the way as if he knew every turn and every path by heart. It was strange because they had never been to this scary place before. Victor, Clara, and Brumble followed him, but Victor felt something wasn't right.

Victor kept watching Gruffle closely. The way Gruffle moved was too confident, like he had been here many times before. Suddenly, as Gruffle shifted his back, Victor saw something shiny on him.

Victor looked closely and saw a black crystal attached to Gruffle's spine. The crystal was glowing faintly, like it was alive. Victor blinked and shook his head, thinking, Am I imagining this?

"Victor, what's wrong?" Clara asked softly, noticing he had slowed down.

"It's nothing... I think," Victor replied, trying to act normal. But deep inside, he felt something was very wrong.

Victor walked back to Brumble, who was walking a little behind. "Brumble," he whispered, trying not to let Gruffle hear, "can you tell me more about this prison we're going to? What kind of place is it?"

Brumble's face became serious. He let out a deep breath before speaking. "Victor, the prison is not like any place you've ever seen. It's full of darkness. It's not just a prison—it's a trap for souls. It's the scariest, most dangerous place in the whole world."

Victor felt a chill run down his spine. "What happens there?" he asked, his voice shaking a little.

Brumble looked straight ahead at Gruffle before lowering his voice even more. "In Noxmire's prison, they don't just lock you up. They take your soul. When someone goes against Noxmire, they are taken to a special chamber. There, the guards make them stand on strange glowing boxes. The guards say some scary magic words and throw shiny crystals into the air. These crystals... they stick to the person and suck their soul out."

Victor's eyes widened. "Suck their soul? What happens to them then?"

Brumble nodded sadly. "The person becomes a puppet. They look alive, but they're not themselves anymore. Their soul gets trapped inside those crystals, and they're forced to serve Noxmire forever. It's worse than death, Victor."

Victor's heart was pounding now. He remembered the black crystal he had seen on Gruffle's back.

"Brumble," Victor said slowly, "have you ever seen a black crystal stuck to someone's body?"

Brumble stopped and stared at Victor, his face turning pale. "What do you mean? Why are you asking that?"

Victor hesitated. He didn't know if he should tell Brumble what he saw. Finally, he said, "I thought I saw something on Gruffle's back... but maybe it's nothing."

Brumble grabbed Victor's arm. "Victor, if you see something strange, you must tell me right away. This place can mess with your mind. It can turn good people bad."

Victor nodded, but he felt more scared now. He looked at Gruffle again, who was still walking confidently ahead as if nothing was wrong.

Victor and Brumble knew something had to be done about the black crystal on Gruffle's back, but they also knew they had to be extremely careful. If Gruffle realized what they were up to, things could go very wrong.

As they walked, Brumble whispered to Victor, "We need to get that crystal off Gruffle without him noticing. It could be controlling him."

Victor nodded. "But how? He'll feel it if we just grab it."

Brumble thought for a moment and then said, "I have an idea. We'll distract him. Clara can help. While he's not paying attention, I'll use my claws to carefully cut it off."

Victor wasn't sure if it would work, but they didn't have another plan. They slowed their pace to walk beside Clara, who had been quiet the whole time. Victor whispered the plan to her, and her eyes widened.

"Are you sure?" Clara asked nervously.

"We don't have a choice," Victor said. "If that crystal is controlling Gruffle, it's dangerous for all of us."

Clara nodded. "Okay, I'll do my best to keep him distracted."

They hurried to catch up with Gruffle, who was walking ahead confidently. Clara called out, "Gruffle! Wait up! I need your help!"

Gruffle stopped and turned around, looking a little confused. "What is it, Clara?"

Clara pretended to stumble and pointed at her shoe. "I think something is stuck here. Can you check it for me? You're stronger than me."

Gruffle sighed and knelt down to look at her shoe. "Really, Clara? We're in the middle of Noxmire's territory, and you're worried about a shoe?"

While Gruffle was busy with Clara, Brumble quickly moved behind him. He motioned for Victor to stay quiet.

Brumble's claws glowed faintly as he carefully reached for the crystal on Gruffle's back.

The crystal was stuck tightly, but Brumble worked quickly and quietly. He used his claws to cut the edges of the crystal where it attached to Gruffle's skin. The crystal made a faint humming sound, and Brumble's eyes narrowed as he concentrated.

Gruffle stood up suddenly, and Brumble froze. "Clara, your shoe is fine. Let's keep moving."

Clara smiled nervously. "Thanks, Gruffle. You're the best!"

Gruffle turned to continue walking, and Brumble gave the crystal one last tug. It came loose with a soft pop, and Brumble quickly hid it behind his back.

Victor let out a silent sigh of relief, but Brumble whispered, "We're not done yet. Let's keep an eye on him and see if anything changes."

Victor and Brumble walked quietly, both deep in thought. They could feel that something wasn't right. Gruffle was acting strange, and they knew in their hearts that this wasn't the real Gruffle.

Victor looked at Brumble, who seemed lost in his own thoughts. "Do you think we're being tricked? Is Gruffle really...?" Victor couldn't finish the sentence. He didn't want to believe it, but deep down, something was off.

Brumble lowered his voice and whispered, "I'm not sure, Victor. But I can feel it too. The way Gruffle is acting... it's not like him. He's leading us straight into Noxmire's prison. This feels like a trap."

Victor's heart sank. They had come so far, fought so many battles, and now they were being led into danger by someone they trusted. But what if Gruffle wasn't in control? What if he was being forced to do this by the black crystal?

Victor clenched his fists. "What if he's being controlled by the crystal? What if he's not really doing this by choice?"

Brumble nodded slowly. "It's possible. The crystal could be affecting his mind. But we can't know for sure unless we do something about it."

Victor thought for a moment. "We have to try. Even if there's a chance this isn't the real Gruffle, we can't let ourselves walk into that prison. We have to take a chance."

Brumble agreed. "We'll be careful. We'll keep our guard up and try to find a way to break the spell. But we need to move fast."

As they walked, they kept a close eye on Gruffle. He was still leading them forward, his movements sure and steady, but his eyes lacked the warmth and kindness Victor had always known. The way he walked, the way he talked—it was all wrong.

Victor felt the weight of the decision they had to make. They were walking into danger, but they couldn't turn back now. They had to figure out what was really happening, even if it meant risking everything.

And then, just as they were about to reach the entrance of Noxmire's prison, something strange happened. Gruffle stopped suddenly and turned to face them. He stared at them with cold eyes that sent a chill down Victor's spine.

"You've figured it out, haven't you?" Gruffle's voice was different now—flat and emotionless. "You know this isn't me."

Victor's heart raced. "What do you mean? What's going on, Gruffle? Why are you acting like this?"

Gruffle didn't answer right away. Instead, he raised his hand to his chest and pulled out the black crystal. "This... this is what's controlling me. It's not my fault."

Brumble stepped forward. "But we can stop this. We can take the crystal from you and break its hold."

Gruffle shook his head slowly. "It's too late. The crystal has already taken too much of me. The real Gruffle is lost."

Victor felt a mix of sadness and anger. He wanted to believe Gruffle, but he also knew they couldn't give up yet. They had come too far. "We're not giving up on you, Gruffle. We'll figure this out. We'll save you."

For a moment, Gruffle's eyes softened, and it looked like he might say something more. But then, a dark shadow seemed to pass over him. His eyes turned cold again, and his voice grew harsh.

"You don't understand," he said. "You never will. You should have stayed away. Now, you're in my world. You're in Noxmire's world."

Before Victor or Brumble could react, Gruffle turned and began walking toward the prison entrance again, the black crystal still glowing faintly in his hand.

Victor and Brumble exchanged a look. There was no turning back now. They had to follow him, not just to save themselves, but to save Gruffle from whatever darkness had taken hold of him.

Gruffle led them into a big, dark room. The room was so quiet they could hear their own breathing. The walls were made of black, shiny stone, and the air smelled strange, like something was burning. In the middle of the room, there were three glowing boxes. Each box was big enough for someone to stand on.

Gruffle smiled and pointed to the boxes. "Stand on those," he said. "That's the only way to move forward."

Victor and Brumble looked at each other. Clara stood close to Victor, her face full of worry. They didn't trust Gruffle anymore. Something felt wrong, but they didn't know what else to do. Slowly, they stepped onto the glowing boxes.

Victor's box felt warm under his feet. A strange, soft light began to glow around him and Brumble. It felt like something was pulling them, but they couldn't tell what it was. Clara stood nearby, too scared to move.

Suddenly, Gruffle started to laugh. But it wasn't his normal laugh. This laugh was deep, cold, and scary. Victor's stomach sank. "What's happening?" he asked, looking at Gruffle.

Gruffle's face started to change. His eyes turned black like the night, and his voice became mean and rough. "You fools!" he said. "Did you really think I was helping you? Ha! I was leading you into a trap!"

Victor's heart started beating very fast. Brumble clenched his fists, ready to fight. "Gruffle! What are you saying?" Brumble asked.

Gruffle—who didn't seem like Gruffle anymore—took a step forward. "I'm not your friend," he said with a sneer. "I work for Noxmire. I am one of his soldiers. And now, your souls will belong to him!"

Victor and Brumble tried to move, but the light from the boxes held them in place. It felt like the boxes were pulling something from inside them, like their energy or their spirit.

Gruffle laughed again. "These boxes will take your souls," he said. "Just like they've done to so many others. You'll become Noxmire's slaves forever!"

Victor gritted his teeth. He looked at Clara, who was frozen with fear. He had to think fast. "Why are you doing this, Gruffle?" Victor asked, trying to stall for time.

Gruffle's grin grew wider. "It's not me," he said. "It's the crystal! The crystal gives me power over you!"

He turned around and reached behind his back to grab the black crystal attached to his spine. But then, his hand froze in mid-air. His grin disappeared, replaced by confusion. He patted his back, searching for the crystal.

But it wasn't there.

Gruffle spun around, his black eyes wide with anger. "Where is it?" he shouted. "Where's the crystal?"

Victor smiled and stepped off the glowing box. He pulled the black crystal out of his pocket and held it up for Gruffle to see. "Looking for this?" Victor said, his voice strong and brave.

Gruffle's face twisted with rage. "How did you get that?" he yelled. "Give it back! You don't know what you're holding!"

Brumble jumped off his box and stood beside Victor. "You've lost, Gruffle—or whoever you are," Brumble said, his voice firm.

Gruffle's black eyes darted around the room, looking for a way to take back the crystal. "You don't understand!" he shouted. "That crystal holds Noxmire's power. Without it, I—"

Victor didn't wait for him to finish. He looked at the crystal in his hand. It was small, shiny, and black as midnight. But it felt heavy, like it was full of something bad. Victor knew what he had to do.

"Brumble, hold him back!" Victor shouted.

Gruffle lunged forward, trying to grab the crystal, but Brumble tackled him to the ground. "Go, Victor!" Brumble yelled. "Destroy it!"

Victor looked around the room for something sharp. He saw a broken piece of stone lying nearby. He grabbed it and placed the crystal on the ground. Gruffle screamed, "No! You can't do this! You'll regret it!"

Victor didn't listen. He raised the stone high and smashed it down onto the crystal. The crystal cracked, and a strange black smoke began to seep out. The room started to shake, and the glowing boxes flickered like candles in the wind.

Gruffle screamed, his voice full of pain and fear. "Stop! You don't know what you're doing!" he cried.

Victor hit the crystal again, harder this time. It shattered into tiny pieces, and the black smoke exploded into the air, swirling around the room like a storm. The shaking stopped, and the glowing boxes went dark.

The room grew quiet. Gruffle lay on the ground, motionless. For a moment, Victor thought it was all over. Then Gruffle stirred. He opened his eyes, and they were no longer black. They were back to normal.

"Victor... Brumble..." Gruffle said weakly. "What happened? Where am I?"

Victor knelt beside him and smiled. "Welcome back, Gruffle," he said. "We missed you."

Brumble helped Gruffle sit up. "We've got a lot to explain," Brumble said.

Before they could say more, the ground beneath them started to rumble again. The walls cracked, and pieces of the ceiling began to fall. "We need to get out of here!" Victor shouted.

They ran toward the exit, dodging falling rocks and jumping over cracks in the floor. The room was collapsing behind them, but they kept running. When they finally made it out, they stopped to catch their breath.

Victor looked at the shattered crystal in his hand. "We did it," he said. "We broke Noxmire's trap."

Brumble patted Victor on the back. "Good job, kid," he said. "But this fight isn't over yet."

Gruffle nodded, his face serious. "Noxmire will know what we've done. He won't stop coming after us."

Victor clenched his fist. "Let him come," he said. "We'll be ready."

The three of them stood together, looking out at the dark land ahead. The fight against Noxmire was far from over, but for the first time, they felt like they had a chance to win.

They weren't just fighting for themselves anymore. They were fighting for everyone who had ever been trapped, hurt, or controlled by Noxmire. And they weren't going to stop until he was defeated.

With new courage in their hearts, they turned and continued their journey. The road ahead was long, but they knew they weren't alone. Together, they were stronger than Noxmire could ever imagine.

As they destroyed the cursed crystal, the entire prison suddenly became silent. No screams, no whispers—just a deep, heavy silence that made their hearts pound faster. The air felt colder, and their footsteps echoed loudly against the stone walls.

Victor, Brumble, Clara, and Gruffle looked around. The prison, which had been filled with eerie sounds and dark shadows, now seemed empty. There were only walls and chambers, but no prisoners, no guards—nothing. It was as if the destruction of the crystal had erased everything.

They continued walking, their eyes scanning the area for any signs of life. As they went deeper into the prison, the air grew heavier, and the walls seemed to close in around them. The dim light from the torches flickered like they were about to go out.

Suddenly, they entered a massive chamber. It was enormous, with high ceilings covered in strange carvings. In the center of the room, they saw something that made them stop in their tracks.

A huge dragon.

The dragon was ancient, with scales as dark as midnight and wings folded tightly against its body. Its head was bowed, and its eyes were closed, as if it were meditating. It sat with its legs crossed, looking calm but powerful. Around the dragon, there were piles of ash and broken chains, as though it had been here for centuries.

Brumble, who always tried to stay brave, stepped forward cautiously. "Hello, mister," he said, his voice trembling slightly. "Can you hear us?"

At first, there was no response. The dragon remained still, its eyes closed. But then, something changed. The air around them grew hotter, and the ground began to shake.

The dragon's eyes snapped open.

Its eyes glowed with fiery light, and from them came streams of flame that looked like fiery ropes. The ropes shot out and wrapped around Victor, Brumble, and Gruffle, lifting them into the air. They couldn't move, and the heat was unbearable.

Clara screamed and tried to run, but the dragon's voice boomed through the chamber. "STOP!" it roared. The sound was so loud that it felt like the walls were shaking.

The dragon turned its fiery gaze toward the three trapped in the air. "Who dares disturb my rest?" it growled, its voice deep and rumbling like thunder. "What do you want, foolish mortals?"

Victor struggled against the fiery ropes but couldn't break free. "We mean no harm!" he shouted. "We're just looking for answers!"

The dragon narrowed its glowing eyes. "Answers?" it said, its tone filled with suspicion. "What answers do you seek?"

Brumble, despite being trapped, managed to speak. "We're here to stop Noxmire!" he said. "We need to find the truth to defeat him!"

The dragon tilted its massive head, the flames around its eyes flickering. "Noxmire," it said slowly, as if the name brought back old memories. "That name has haunted this land for ages. Why do you think you, mere mortals, can defeat him?"

Victor clenched his fists. "Because we have to!" he said. "He's hurt too many people. He's taken too much. We can't let him win!"

The dragon stared at Victor for a long moment. Then it laughed—a deep, echoing laugh that filled the chamber. "Brave words," it said. "But bravery is not enough. You will need more than courage to face Noxmire."

The dragon released its fiery ropes, and the three of them fell to the ground with a thud. Clara ran to Victor's side, helping him up.

The dragon leaned down, its massive face just inches away from Victor. "You've destroyed the cursed crystal," it said. "That is no small feat. Perhaps there is more to you than meets the eye."

Victor stood up, brushing off the ash on his clothes. "Will you help us?" he asked. "Do you know how to defeat Noxmire?"

The dragon pulled back and sat upright again. "Help you?" it said. "I do not help lightly. But perhaps I can offer you... a test."

Brumble frowned. "A test?" he said. "What kind of test?"

The dragon's eyes glowed brighter. "If you wish to defeat Noxmire, you must prove your worth," it said. "There is a chamber beyond this one. Inside, you will find three challenges. Complete them, and I will give you the knowledge you seek. Fail, and you will never leave this place."

Victor looked at the others. Clara was nervous but nodded. Brumble and Gruffle exchanged glances, then nodded as well.

"We'll do it," Victor said firmly.

The dragon let out a small puff of smoke. "Very well," it said. "But remember: not all who enter the chamber return."

It raised one massive claw and slammed it onto the ground. The room shook, and a hidden door in the wall creaked open, revealing a dark passage. The dragon gestured toward it with its claw.

"Enter," it said. "And let the test begin."

Victor took a deep breath and stepped forward, leading the group toward the dark passage. The dragon watched them go, its fiery eyes glowing with a strange, unreadable expression.

"Good luck," it whispered. "You will need it."

13

As Victor, Clara, Brumble, and Gruffle stepped through the dark passageway, the air grew colder with each step. The heavy stone door behind them slammed shut with an echoing thud, trapping them inside. The sound reverberated through the darkness, making Clara shiver.

"This place feels alive," Clara whispered, her voice trembling.

"Alive and dangerous," Brumble muttered. The faint glow of ancient runes on the walls cast eerie shadows, and the flickering light seemed to follow their movements. "Be on your guard. We don't know what's waiting for us."

The passage led them to a large, circular chamber with three towering doorways. Each door bore a glowing symbol: a fist, a brain, and a heart. Above the doors, carved into the stone, was a riddle:

"Strength, Mind, Heart. Prove each, or perish."

Victor read the words aloud. "Strength, mind, and heart. These must be the challenges the dragon spoke of."

Gruffle studied the doors, his eyes narrowing. "Each door will test something different. We need to pass all three to move forward."

Clara looked nervous. "What happens if we fail?"

Brumble gave her a grim look. "We don't fail. That's not an option."

Victor stepped forward, determination etched on his face. "Let's start with the first door."

Challenge One: Strength

The door with the glowing fist symbol creaked open, revealing a vast stone room. The ceiling was impossibly high, and the air felt heavy, as if the room itself was pressing down on them. At the center of the chamber stood a massive, stone creature—a golem. Its jagged body towered over them, and in its hands, it held a hammer so large it seemed impossible to lift.

The golem's eyes glowed red as it turned to face them. With a low, grinding roar, it raised its hammer, and the ground trembled beneath their feet.

Clara gasped. "What is that thing?!"

Brumble stepped forward, his voice steady but tense. "A guardian. Made of pure stone. And it's not here to greet us."

The golem took a step forward, each movement sending vibrations through the room. It swung its hammer, narrowly missing Victor and smashing into the ground, leaving a crater.

Victor quickly scanned the room. There were large boulders scattered around, as well as chains hanging from the ceiling. He turned to the others. "We can't fight it directly. It's too strong. But we can use the room to our advantage."

"What's the plan?" Gruffle asked.

Victor pointed to one of the chains. "We'll set a trap. Clara and Brumble, you distract it. Gruffle and I will tie one of those chains to a boulder and swing it at the golem."

Clara and Brumble exchanged nervous glances but nodded. They ran to opposite sides of the room, shouting and waving their arms to get the golem's attention. The creature roared and turned toward them, swinging its hammer wildly.

Meanwhile, Victor and Gruffle worked quickly to tie a chain around one of the largest boulders. The boulder was heavy, and their hands trembled as they struggled to secure the chain.

"Hurry!" Clara shouted as the golem's hammer smashed dangerously close to her.

"Almost there," Victor grunted. Finally, they secured the chain and pulled with all their might. The boulder swung into the air, crashing into the golem's chest. The impact sent cracks spreading across its stone body.

"Now!" Victor yelled. The four of them charged at the weakened golem, pushing with all their strength. The creature toppled backward, shattering into pieces as it hit the ground.

Breathing heavily, they stood over the broken remains. "One challenge down," Victor said. "Two to go."

Challenge Two: Mind

The second door opened into a room unlike any they had seen before. The walls, ceiling, and floor were covered in mirrors, creating an endless maze of reflections. At the center of the room was a pedestal holding a glowing orb.

Clara stepped forward cautiously. "What's this supposed to be?"

Before anyone could answer, the mirrors began to shift. The reflections twisted and multiplied, creating illusions that made it impossible to tell what was real. The pedestal and orb appeared in multiple places, each one looking identical.

"It's a puzzle," Gruffle said. "But it won't be easy."

Victor frowned. "We need to figure out which orb is real."

Brumble stroked his beard. "Mirrors show what's there, but not always where it is. There must be a trick."

Clara's eyes lit up. "Wait! Look at the light." She pointed to the beams of light reflecting off the orb. "The real orb's light won't reflect like the fake ones. We just have to follow the light."

The group carefully observed the reflections, noticing that one beam of light didn't behave like the others. Slowly, they followed it to a pedestal in the corner of the room. Victor reached out and touched the orb.

The mirrors stopped shifting, and the room returned to normal. They had passed the second challenge.

Challenge Three: Heart

The final doorway led to a dark, quiet room. At first, it seemed empty, but a soft glow appeared in the center. Floating in the light was a small, golden box.

As they approached, voices began to echo in the room. They weren't ordinary voices; they sounded like memories. Victor heard his parents calling his name. Clara heard her sister's laughter. Brumble and Gruffle heard voices from their childhood, filled with joy and sorrow.

The box's glow intensified, and the voices grew louder. Then, a question echoed through the room: "What matters most to you?"

Victor stepped forward, his heart heavy. "Family," he said softly. "Love. Protecting the people I care about."

Clara wiped a tear from her eye. "Helping others," she said. "Making the world better."

Brumble and Gruffle added their own answers, speaking of courage, loyalty, and the bonds that kept them strong. As they spoke, the box glowed brighter, and the voices faded away. The light wrapped around them, warm and reassuring.

"You have passed," the voice said. "Go forth with the strength of your hearts."

The group stumbled out of the final chamber, exhausted but victorious. They found themselves back in the dragon's lair, where the ancient creature waited. Its fiery eyes flickered with approval.

"You have proven yourselves," the dragon rumbled. "Now, I will give you what you seek."

The dragon lowered its head and whispered ancient words. A glowing map appeared in the air, pointing them toward their next destination—the place where Noxmire could finally be defeated.

The old dragon, towering over them with an aura of wisdom and power, softened his fiery gaze as he saw the determination in their eyes. His massive wings folded gently behind him, and he leaned closer, his deep voice echoing through the chamber.

"You have proven yourselves worthy," the dragon rumbled, his tone both commanding and warm. "Few have the courage to face the challenges of this cursed place and live to tell the tale."

The group stood in awe, catching their breath after the trials. Brumble, ever the bold one, stepped forward, bowing respectfully. "Who are you, mighty dragon? And why are you here, imprisoned in this dark chamber?"

The dragon straightened his posture, his scales shimmering faintly in the dim light. "I am Milo-Blaze," he began, his voice reverberating. "Blaze is the name given to me by the Great Drake himself, a name that signifies my fiery spirit and undying loyalty. 'Milo' is a title bestowed upon those who served Drake, guardians of his realm and protectors of his light."

Victor's eyes widened. "You knew Drake?" he asked, his voice filled with curiosity and hope.

Milo-Blaze nodded solemnly. "Yes, I was not only his ally but his closest confidant. Drake was more than a leader; he was the heart of Drakoria. His kindness and wisdom were unmatched, a beacon of light in a world that now lies in darkness."

Clara took a step closer, her voice trembling with excitement. "Does that mean... is Drake still alive?"

The dragon's fiery eyes softened, and he let out a deep sigh. "Indeed, Drake lives. But he is not as you might imagine. After the invasion of Drakoria by the accursed Noxmire, Drake sacrificed himself to seal the last remnants of pure energy in this world. His body rests, hidden in a place only a true Milo can find, but his soul lingers, intertwined with the fabric of this realm, waiting for the day the darkness is purged."

Brumble, his chest puffed with pride, asked, "And you, Milo-Blaze? Why are you here, trapped for centuries?"

Milo-Blaze's gaze grew distant, memories flooding his mind. "When Noxmire's army stormed Drakoria, I fought alongside Drake and the others. We were outnumbered but determined to protect our home. As the battle raged, I was tasked with safeguarding the secrets of Drakoria—secrets that could either save us or destroy us if they fell into the wrong hands. In my final battle, I was wounded and forced into hiding. This chamber became my prison, but also my sanctuary. For centuries, I have waited for someone worthy to continue what we could not finish."

Victor clenched his fists. "We will finish it," he said firmly. "We'll find Drake, defeat Noxmire, and restore Drakoria to what it once was."

Milo-Blaze studied Victor, his fiery gaze penetrating as if reading the depths of his soul. "You carry the determination of your ancestors," he said, his voice heavy with meaning.

"But this path will not be easy. Noxmire is not just a foe of flesh and blood; he is a force of darkness, feeding on fear and despair. To defeat him, you must be stronger than his hatred, braver than his shadows."

Clara, her voice filled with resolve, asked, "What do we need to do?"

Milo-Blaze unfolded his massive wings, the chamber trembling as he did. "You must first find the Heart of Drakoria," he said. "It is the key to awakening Drake. But beware, the Heart is hidden in the Valley of Echoes, a place where the past comes alive, and every step is fraught with danger. Only those pure of heart can retrieve it."

Brumble nodded. "We will go. Together, we can face whatever lies ahead."

Milo-Blaze gave a solemn nod. "But before you leave," he said, "take this." He extended one of his claws, revealing a glowing shard of crystal. "This is a fragment of Drake's light, a piece of his essence. It will guide you when all seems lost. Protect it with your lives."

Victor carefully took the shard, feeling its warmth in his hands. It pulsed faintly, as if alive. "Thank you, Milo-Blaze," he said earnestly. "We won't let you or Drake down."

The dragon's fiery eyes flickered with a hint of a smile. "Go now, brave ones. The fate of Drakoria rests in your hands."

As they turned to leave, Milo-Blaze called out, his voice echoing like thunder. "Remember, the shadows will try to deceive you, to break you. But trust in each other, and you will find the strength to overcome."

With newfound determination, Victor, Clara, Brumble, and the real Gruffle—who had proven his loyalty in the trials—set off, ready to face the next chapter of their perilous journey. Behind them, Milo-Blaze watched, his heart swelling with hope for the first time in centuries.

Milo Blaze further said, "There is indeed a way to destroy Noxmire, but it will not be easy. Centuries ago, a sacred text was created—The Holy Drake Book. It has remained closed, untouched by mortal hands for ages. This book has the ability to trap the spirits of evil, but only if the conditions are right."

He paused, allowing the weight of his words to sink in.

"To begin, you must extract the crystal embedded in Noxmire's back. Once you have it, place it upon the Holy Drake Book. That will open it, and when it does, it will trap Noxmire's spirit forever. But beware—the book's power is immense, and unlocking it will require great strength of will."

Brumble frowned. "And after we trap Noxmire's spirit, then what?"

Milo-Blaze's eyes narrowed, reflecting both the hope and danger of what was to come. "Once the book is closed again, it will reveal the location of the Obsidian Compass. The Obsidian Compass is no mere artifact—it is the key to closing the portals that connect all the realms, trapping Noxmire's dark influence and preventing him from escaping back into the worlds he has corrupted."

Victor stood tall, the crystal from Milo-Blaze still glowing in his hand. "We will do it. We'll find the book, trap Noxmire, and destroy the compass. This ends now."

Milo-Blaze nodded approvingly, his fiery gaze proud but somber. "Remember, the path ahead is fraught with peril. The Holy Drake Book cannot be easily found, and Noxmire will do everything in his power to stop you. Stay vigilant, trust in each other, and you may just succeed."

Clara placed a hand on Victor's shoulder. "We'll face whatever comes together. No matter the cost."

With that, the group set off once again, their determination stronger than ever. They knew that the fate of all worlds rested on their shoulders—and the time to stop Noxmire was drawing near.

The Jungle Adventure Begins

Victor, Clara, Brumble, and Gruffle had been walking for hours. They had followed the map that Milo-Blaze gave them, and it had led them into the heart of a thick jungle. Tall trees reached high into the sky, their leaves so big they seemed like umbrellas. The ground was soft and muddy, and strange noises echoed all around them. Birds with bright feathers flew by, and little animals scurried through the bushes.

The jungle was beautiful, but it was also mysterious. It felt like the kind of place where anything could happen. The air was hot and sticky, making everyone feel a little tired. But they knew they couldn't stop. They were on a mission to find the Holy Drake Book, and this jungle was part of the journey.

Brumble was the first to speak. He was always the brave one, charging ahead with his usual excitement. "Come on, everyone! This jungle's not so scary. We just need to keep moving!"

Clara, walking beside Victor, nodded but felt a little nervous. She had never been in a jungle this big before. She looked at the map again, trying to make sense of the path ahead.

"It says we need to find a dragon's friend," she said quietly. "But how are we going to do that?"

Victor looked at her with a reassuring smile. "We'll figure it out. We always do. And don't forget—we have each other."

Clara smiled back, feeling a little braver.

They walked on, moving slowly and carefully. The jungle was dense, with vines hanging down like ropes and thick bushes that seemed to close in around them. As they moved through the jungle, they had to watch out for anything dangerous. The map didn't say much about what kind of creatures or plants they might meet, but they knew it wasn't going to be easy.

Suddenly, Brumble stopped. "Wait," he said, holding up his hand. "I think I saw something shiny over there!"

The group followed his gaze, and there, in the middle of a patch of colorful flowers, was a plant with glowing petals. The flower shimmered with a soft light, like it was made of stars. It looked so beautiful that Clara couldn't help but step closer to it.

"Look at that!" she said, her eyes wide with wonder. "It's so pretty!"

Brumble looked at it, but his face suddenly turned serious. "Clara, don't touch it! That plant is dangerous!"

But it was too late. Clara, mesmerized by the flower's beauty, reached out and plucked it from the ground.

The moment her fingers touched the petals, the jungle around them seemed to change. The air felt heavier, and a strange hum filled the air. Clara felt a tingling sensation on her skin, and her hand started to itch. She pulled the flower away, but the tingling wouldn't stop.

Victor rushed to her side. "Clara, what's wrong? Are you okay?"

Clara blinked, trying to clear her head. "I—I don't know. My hand itches, and I feel... strange."

Brumble's face turned pale. "Clara, you've touched the Death's Bloom! It's one of the most dangerous plants in this jungle. Its touch can make you sick—really sick."

Clara looked down at the flower in her hand, its petals now curling up like sharp claws. "What do we do?"

Brumble didn't waste any time. "We have to find an antidote fast. If we don't, the poison could spread and make you paralyzed! We need to get you to a special herb that can stop it."

Victor helped Clara sit down on a rock. "Don't worry, Clara. We'll find the antidote. We've faced tough things before, and we can do it again."

Gruffle, who had been standing quietly, sniffed the air. "I can smell something... It's faint, but I think I know where the antidote might be."

Brumble turned to him. "Where? Tell us, Gruffle!"

Gruffle's ears twitched. "There's a small clearing to the left. It's hidden, but I can smell the herb we need. Follow me."

With no time to lose, the group followed Gruffle through the jungle, moving quickly but carefully. Clara held onto Victor's arm for support, feeling weaker with each step. The map didn't show any special places or helpful hints, but they knew they had to keep going.

After what felt like forever, they reached a small clearing. It was quieter here. The sounds of the jungle seemed distant, as if the trees themselves were holding their breath. In the center of the clearing was a patch of plants that looked much different from the dangerous flower Clara had touched. These plants were green and full of life, with leaves that glowed faintly in the dim light. One plant in particular had large, round leaves with a soft blue color.

"This is it," Gruffle said, pointing to the plant. "This is the antidote. It's called Moonleaf. The leaves can heal poison."

Brumble quickly knelt down and picked several of the Moonleaf leaves. "We need to mash these up and mix them with water," he said. "That should help Clara."

Victor helped Brumble gather the leaves, and soon they had a small paste made from the plants. They made Clara drink the mixture, and she winced at the bitter taste. It wasn't pleasant, but she didn't care. She just wanted the strange feeling in her body to go away.

Minutes passed. At first, Clara didn't feel any different. But slowly, the tingling in her hand began to fade, and the dizziness started to lift. Her vision cleared, and her breath felt easier.

Victor smiled at her. "How do you feel?"

Clara touched her hand and nodded. "Much better. I think the antidote worked."

Brumble grinned. "See? Told you we could handle it."

But Clara didn't take her eyes off the clearing. The jungle had been full of surprises, and she had learned an important lesson: not everything that looked pretty was safe. "We have to be careful," she said. "We can't let our guard down."

Victor nodded, looking around. "You're right. We've come a long way, but we're not done yet."

With Clara feeling better, the group continued their journey through the jungle. They didn't know what other dangers lay ahead, but they knew they had each other—and that made them stronger.

Clara felt much better after taking the antidote, but the jungle still felt just as mysterious and full of hidden dangers. The group, now more cautious, pressed forward, sticking together and watching for any signs of trouble. They kept their eyes on the map that Milo-Blaze had given them, hoping it would lead them to safety.

The sun was beginning to set, casting a golden light over the jungle. The air grew cooler, and the strange noises of the jungle seemed to grow louder as night approached. A soft breeze rustled the leaves, and fireflies started to light up the darkening forest like tiny stars.

"Do you think we're close?" Clara asked, glancing at Victor. "The map says we need to find a dragon's friend. But how are we supposed to do that?"

Victor looked at the map carefully. "It's not clear yet, but we'll keep going. The map said it would be hard, but we can do it. We've already faced so much."

Brumble, who had been walking ahead, turned back to them. "Hey, I think I see something up ahead. Maybe it's the dragon we need to befriend."

Everyone stopped and followed Brumble, who was already moving faster toward what he had spotted. The group soon reached a large clearing. In the center of the clearing stood a giant rock formation, and perched on top was a massive dragon. Its scales shimmered in the fading sunlight, and its wings were spread wide, making it look even bigger. The dragon was watching them with fiery eyes.

"Wow," Clara whispered. "It's huge."

Brumble took a step forward, his voice full of confidence. "Hello, mighty dragon! We've come seeking your help!"

The dragon's fiery eyes locked onto Brumble. It didn't move, just watched them quietly. Its massive claws gripped the rock beneath it, and for a moment, the jungle felt still.

Victor stepped forward, trying to speak calmly. "We mean you no harm, great dragon. We need your help to find a portal. If you help us, we will help you in return."

The dragon's gaze shifted between the group, sizing them up. Then, slowly, it spoke, its voice deep and rumbling, like the sound of thunder.

"Why should I help you, little ones?" the dragon asked, its eyes narrowing. "What do you have to offer me?"

Brumble didn't hesitate. He stood tall and said, "We are on a quest to stop Noxmire, the dark force that has been threatening this world. We have come to find the Holy Drake Book, and we need your help to find a portal that will lead us to Noxmire's palace. If you help us, we will make sure Noxmire's evil is stopped once and for all."

The dragon's eyes glowed brighter as it considered Brumble's words. "You speak of Noxmire? The one who has brought darkness to this world?" it rumbled, its voice almost like a growl.

"Yes," Victor replied, his voice steady. "We need to stop him, and we believe you can help us."

The dragon stood silently for a long moment, its wings flicking slightly. The jungle seemed to hold its breath as the dragon studied them. Then, finally, it spoke again.

"Very well," it said, its voice softening. "I will help you. But know this—befriending a dragon is not easy. You must prove your courage, your loyalty, and your strength. If you can do that, I will help you find the portal. But fail, and you will not be allowed to pass."

Clara felt her heart race. "What do we need to do?"

The dragon's fiery eyes seemed to glow even brighter. "You must face me in a test of strength and wit. You must show that you are worthy of my trust. Only then will I take you to the portal."

Brumble stepped forward, his usual confidence turning into determination. "We'll do whatever it takes. We won't fail."

The dragon lowered its massive head, bringing its fiery eyes level with the group. "Then let the test begin."

The Test of Courage

The dragon's voice boomed in the jungle, and before anyone could react, the air around them began to change. The ground trembled beneath their feet, and a thick fog suddenly appeared, swirling around them. The jungle that had seemed so familiar just moments before now looked completely different. The trees were twisted, the shadows longer, and the air was heavy with an eerie silence.

The dragon's voice echoed through the fog. "In order to pass this test, you must find your way through the Mist of Doubt. Many have entered and never returned. The fog will confuse you, and the shadows will try to trick you. You must trust each other and keep moving forward. Only then will you find the way."

Victor looked around, trying to make sense of the thick fog that now surrounded them. "We need to stay together," he said, his voice steady but nervous. "If we stick together, we can do this."

Clara, Brumble, and Gruffle nodded. They didn't have a choice. They had to pass the test if they wanted to continue their journey.

As they walked through the fog, they soon began to feel the weight of the jungle's strange magic. The mist made everything look blurry, and the sounds of the jungle seemed far away. At times, they heard voices—whispers that sounded like their own. The shadows seemed to move, making it hard to tell where they were going.

"This is creepy," Clara whispered, gripping Victor's arm.

"We can do this," Victor said, trying to reassure her. "Stay close and trust each other."

Brumble, ever the bold one, led the way, his eyes scanning the mist for any signs of danger. "Don't let the shadows get to you," he said. "We've faced worse than this before."

But the deeper they went, the harder it became to see. The fog thickened, and the whispers grew louder. They seemed to come from all directions, confusing them.

"Why are we doing this?" Clara asked, her voice filled with doubt. "Is it worth it?"

Victor stopped and turned to her, his face serious but kind. "Clara, we're doing this because we have to. Noxmire's darkness is spreading, and we're the only ones who can stop it. We can't give up now."

Clara nodded, but she still felt a little afraid. She took a deep breath and tried to focus on the sound of Victor's voice. They kept moving through the fog, walking slowly but surely.

As they continued, the fog began to clear, and they saw a glowing light in the distance. It was faint, but it was enough to give them hope. Together, they moved toward the light, and slowly, the jungle around them returned to normal. The mist disappeared, and the path ahead became clear.

"Congratulations," the dragon's voice boomed. "You have passed the test of courage. You have shown that you trust each other and can face your fears. I will now help you find the portal."

The dragon, now their ally, led the way through the jungle with great speed, his wings beating the air like thunder. His massive form seemed to part the fog and shadows as if they were nothing. As they moved deeper into the jungle, the shadows began to grow darker, swirling around them like menacing figures.

"Stay close," the dragon's deep voice called. "The shadows will try to break your courage. But I will protect you."

Victor, Clara, Brumble, and Gruffle nodded, their hearts filled with both fear and determination. They had already faced so many challenges, but this was different. They had no idea what dangers awaited them on the other side of the portal.

As they moved forward, the shadows began to shift and writhe, becoming more than just dark shapes. They grew into twisted, evil creatures—creatures made of pure darkness. Their eyes glowed like burning embers, and their claws reached out to grab anything in their path.

"Look out!" Brumble shouted, his voice sharp with warning.

The first shadow creature lunged toward them, its claws slicing through the air. But before it could reach them, the dragon spread his wings wide and roared. The sound was deafening, shaking the very ground beneath them. The shadow creature screeched and was blasted back into the darkness, vanishing with a puff of smoke.

"That's one down," the dragon said calmly. "But there will be more. Keep your wits about you."

The group stayed close to the dragon as they continued moving forward. More shadow creatures emerged from the darkness, their twisted forms snapping and snarling. But each time, the dragon's fiery breath sent them fleeing, and his mighty wings swept the air, blowing them away.

Brumble grinned, his confidence growing with every battle. "These creatures are no match for us!" he declared.

But Clara felt a twinge of doubt. The creatures were getting more and more powerful, and she could feel their evil energy pressing against her. The air felt thick and heavy, as if the very jungle around them was turning against them.

"I don't know how much longer I can do this," Clara said softly, her voice shaking. "It feels like the jungle is alive with darkness."

Victor placed a hand on her shoulder. "We can't stop now, Clara. We've come too far. We have to face this darkness, or we'll never get to Noxmire."

The dragon gave them a reassuring look. "You have more courage than you think. Together, you will defeat this darkness."

And together, they did. With every shadow that appeared, the dragon fought bravely, using his fire and strength to destroy them. The group stayed close, following the dragon and staying strong, knowing they were almost there.

At last, they reached the edge of a cliff. Below them, a swirling vortex of dark energy glowed, its power pulsing with an ominous hum. The portal to Noxmire's palace.

"This is it," the dragon said, his voice heavy with warning. "Once you step through this portal, there is no turning back. Noxmire's palace is a place of endless darkness and terror. You must be ready for anything."

Victor, Clara, Brumble, and Gruffle stood at the edge of the cliff, looking down at the swirling vortex below. They knew this was the moment. The moment they would face Noxmire and put an end to his evil.

"We're ready," Victor said, his voice full of determination. "We'll do whatever it takes."

"Let's go," Brumble added, his eyes shining with bravery.

The dragon gave them one last look before nodding. "Then go. May the light of Drake guide you."

But before they could step forward, the dragon stopped them. He reached into the folds of his wings and produced a small vial of glowing liquid.

"Take this," the dragon said, holding the vial out to Victor. "This liquid will allow you to take on the appearance of Noxmire's guards. You will be able to pass through his palace without being detected. But remember, the effect will only last for one day. After that, your true forms will return. Use this time wisely."

Victor looked at the vial, then at the dragon. "Thank you. This will help us get closer to Noxmire."

Each of them took a sip of the glowing liquid, feeling a strange warmth spread through their bodies. For a moment, they felt dizzy, as though the world was spinning around them. When the feeling passed, they looked at each other in amazement.

They were no longer themselves.

Clara looked at her hands and gasped. Her skin had turned a dark shade, and she felt the power of Noxmire's minions flowing through her. She glanced at Victor, Brumble, and Gruffle, and saw that they had all changed too. Their forms now resembled the dark, imposing figures of Noxmire's palace guards, with armored suits and blackened faces that could intimidate anyone.

"It worked," Victor said, his voice slightly deeper now. "We look just like them."

The dragon nodded. "You are now ready. Go, and remember—the portal will only stay open for a short time. You must act quickly once inside."

With that, the group stepped forward and entered the swirling vortex.

14

The group stepped through the swirling vortex and into Noxmire's palace. Immediately, the oppressive atmosphere hit them. It was cold, dark, and foreboding, like stepping into a nightmare. The towering walls around them were made of black stone, with twisted, jagged designs carved into every surface. The air was thick with the scent of decay and a faint, ominous hum echoed through the halls.

Victor, Clara, Brumble, and Gruffle—all dressed in the dark, imposing armor of Noxmire's guards—walked cautiously through the corridors. The palace seemed to stretch endlessly in every direction, the walls closing in on them as though the place itself was alive. Shadows danced along the walls, and strange, unsettling noises came from all around.

The map the dragon had given them guided their path, but they had little time. The dragon's liquid had given them the appearance of Noxmire's minions for only one day, and they had to find the Holy Drake Book before that time ran out. The book was their key to trapping Noxmire's spirit, and without it, their mission would be doomed.

As they moved deeper into the palace, they encountered a few of Noxmire's real guards. They were tall, dark creatures with glowing red eyes, wearing twisted armor that looked like it had been forged from the very shadows themselves. The guards stared at them suspiciously, but the group held their breath and did their best to act like they belonged.

"Stay calm," Victor whispered. "We don't want to blow our cover."

Clara nodded, her heart racing. "We need to find that book quickly. We can't afford to be discovered."

Brumble, always ready for a challenge, gave a confident nod. "We'll find it. I can feel it in my bones. The book's not far."

The shadows seemed to grow thicker, and strange whispers filled the air, making it hard for them to focus. They turned another corner and found themselves facing a large, ornate door. It was unlike anything they had seen so far—its surface was covered in intricate symbols that seemed to glow faintly in the dim light.

"This is it," Victor said, his voice filled with awe. "This must be where the Holy Drake Book is kept."

Clara stepped forward, her hand trembling as she reached out to push the door open. But just as her fingers touched the cold, black surface, a voice echoed through the hall, low and menacing.

"Who goes there?" it boomed, and the group froze.

From the shadows emerged a figure—a towering, armored guard with glowing red eyes. His voice was deep and full of authority, and the power emanating from him was unmistakable.

"We are new recruits, sir," Victor said quickly, his voice steady despite the fear coursing through him. "Sent to help patrol the palace."

The guard looked them over, his red eyes narrowing. For a moment, the group held their breath, waiting for him to spot something amiss. But finally, the guard gave a grunt of approval.

"Very well," he said. "Make sure you do your duty. No one is allowed near the Holy Drake Book without permission. The master does not take kindly to intruders."

The group nodded quickly, trying to act as normal as possible. "Of course, sir," Clara said, her voice steady even though her heart was pounding.

The guard gave them one last look before turning and disappearing into the shadows.

"That was close," Brumble whispered, exhaling a breath he didn't realize he was holding.

Victor nodded, turning back to the door. "Now let's get that book before we run out of time."

With a quiet push, the door creaked open. Beyond it lay a massive chamber, illuminated by flickering torches that cast eerie shadows along the walls. In the center of the room stood an ancient pedestal, and atop it rested the Holy Drake Book. Its pages were bound in shimmering scales that reflected the dim light, and an aura of power surrounded it, making it seem almost alive.

The group moved cautiously toward the book, their footsteps muffled by the thick carpet of shadows that covered the floor. As they approached the pedestal, the room seemed to grow colder, the air thick with the weight of ancient magic.

"That's it," Clara said softly, her voice full of awe. "The Holy Drake Book."

Victor nodded. "We don't have much time. We need to open it and get the crystal from Noxmire's back, but first, we need to know how to activate it."

Brumble reached out to touch the book, but before his fingers could brush its surface, a low growl echoed from the far corner of the room.

The group turned to see a shadow moving toward them. It was a figure cloaked in darkness, its red eyes glowing from within the blackness. The figure stepped into the light, revealing a tall, gaunt man dressed in dark armor.

"You think you can just take the Holy Drake Book?" the figure hissed, his voice like a snake's. "You are fools. This book is bound by magic far stronger than you can comprehend."

The man's form rippled, and before they could react, he lunged at them with the speed of a shadow, his claws extended like daggers. The group barely managed to jump back in time, but the figure's dark presence was overwhelming, pressing in on them from all sides.

"We don't have time for this," Victor said, his voice filled with urgency. "We need to get the book, and fast."

The dark figure let out a laugh, low and mocking. "You may have entered this place, but you will never leave it with the book. Noxmire's power is greater than any of you can imagine."

Victor gritted his teeth, his determination rising. "We've come too far to fail now."

The group knew they had no time to lose. The Holy Drake Book was now within reach, but the dark figure they'd encountered had made it clear that getting it would not be easy. With their hearts pounding and the weight of their mission pressing on them, Victor made a quick decision.

"Brumble, Clara, Gruffle," he said in a low voice, "You stay here. Distract him and the others. Tell them you're new recruits who don't know the palace's rules or anything about the book."

Brumble grinned, eager for the challenge. "Leave it to me. I'll keep them busy."

Clara, though still uneasy, nodded in agreement. "We'll handle this. Just go—find Noxmire, and get the information we need."

Victor gave them a determined look. "Keep your cover, and don't let them get suspicious. We'll be back as soon as we can."

With that, Victor and Gruffle slipped out of the chamber and into the dark halls of the palace. They were careful not to draw attention, using the shadows to blend in with the other Noxmire guards.

Meanwhile, back in the chamber with the book, Brumble and Clara stood their ground, waiting for the dark figure's next move. He was still glaring at them from the corner, his eyes burning with suspicion.

"New recruits, eh?" he sneered. "I can see it in your eyes—you've never stepped foot in this palace before. What are you really after?"

Brumble quickly put on a confused expression. "Oh, we don't know much yet, sir," he stammered. "We were just assigned here. Still learning the ropes."

Clara nodded in agreement, trying to sound as naive as possible. "Yes, we were just told to guard this chamber. We don't even know what's inside, honestly."

The dark figure tilted his head, his red eyes narrowing as he studied them. He seemed to be weighing their words, trying to decide if they were lying. But Clara and Brumble stood tall, doing their best to keep their composure.

"Well, keep your distance from the book," the figure growled. "It's not for the likes of you to touch. Stay here and stay out of trouble, or you'll regret it."

Brumble swallowed, his voice still acting surprised. "Of course, sir. We'll stay away from the book. We won't cause any trouble."

The figure gave a dismissive wave and turned to walk back into the shadows, his presence lingering in the air like a dark storm cloud. Clara and Brumble let out a collective sigh of relief as he disappeared into the darkness.

"That was too close," Clara whispered. "We need to make sure they don't find out what we're really after."

Brumble nodded. "Agreed. But for now, we just stay here and wait."

Meanwhile, Victor and Gruffle were weaving through the palace, staying out of sight from the other guards. The palace was vast, its corridors stretching endlessly. They knew the book was a crucial step in their mission, but they also had to find Noxmire and learn his weaknesses.

The map from the dragon had led them to this place, but now, they had to find Noxmire himself. If they were going to defeat him and end his reign of darkness, they had to know where he was hiding—and how to get to him.

After a while, they stumbled upon a group of Noxmire's soldiers walking down the hallway. Their armor glinted in the dim light, and their faces were twisted with malice. They didn't look like they cared much about anything except serving Noxmire's dark will.

Victor and Gruffle exchanged a glance. They needed to blend in, and fast.

"Let's join them," Victor whispered, motioning to the group. "We'll find out where Noxmire is."

Gruffle nodded, his expression serious. "We can't mess this up. Stay in character."

The two of them quickly fell into line behind the group of soldiers. The others didn't seem to notice them at first, and Victor was careful to adopt the same cold, distant expression that the other guards wore. Gruffle did the same, his usual friendly demeanor replaced by a hardened look.

As they moved deeper into the palace, the soldiers began to talk, their voices low and murmuring.

"I heard Noxmire's planning something big," one of the guards said. "He's got a new weapon, something even stronger than his shadows."

"Great," another guard replied, "because we definitely need more power. Those pesky rebels keep getting in the way."

Victor and Gruffle exchanged looks. The mention of Noxmire's new weapon piqued their interest. They had to learn more.

"What do you think he's planning?" Gruffle whispered, his voice low.

Victor shook his head. "I'm not sure, but we need to find out."

The group continued walking, eventually coming to a large set of double doors at the end of a long hallway. The soldiers stopped in front of the doors and one of them knocked three times, a low and hollow sound.

After a moment, the doors creaked open, revealing a room bathed in dim red light. Inside, they could see Noxmire—his pale, twisted figure sitting on a throne made of black stone. His eyes were glowing like fiery pits, and the air around him seemed to vibrate with dark energy.

Victor's heart pounded. They had found him. Noxmire was right there.

The soldiers in the group saluted Noxmire, bowing low before him. "My lord," one of them said, "we have brought new recruits. They've been assigned to guard the palace."

Noxmire looked down at them with a cold, piercing gaze. His voice was low and menacing. "Very well. Let them stay. I have more important matters to attend to."

Victor and Gruffle stood still, careful not to draw attention. Noxmire seemed distracted, his attention fixed on something in the distance. This was their chance.

"We need to get closer," Victor whispered. "We have to learn his plans."

Gruffle nodded. "Stay close, but be careful. If he sees us, everything will be over."

The two of them began to move quietly toward Noxmire, trying to stay hidden in the shadows. They could hear his voice—soft but full of authority—as he muttered to himself about his next steps.

"We can't let him finish whatever he's planning," Victor said. "We need to stop him now."

As they inched closer, Victor's mind raced. Time was running out. They had to find a way to defeat Noxmire—and they had to do it quickly.

Victor's mind was racing as he thought of the perfect plan. He quickly turned to Gruffle, his eyes gleaming with determination. "We've got our chance," Victor whispered. "Noxmire's planning something big. I overheard his soldiers talking about a gathering. He's going to address everyone, and that's when we'll make our move."

Gruffle raised an eyebrow, clearly impressed by the sudden turn of events. "A gathering? So everyone will be there?"

Victor nodded. "Yes. Noxmire's going to make some kind of announcement. It's the perfect time to strike. We'll have the whole palace distracted."

Without wasting any time, Victor and Gruffle made their way back to the chamber where Brumble and Clara were still keeping watch over the Holy Drake Book. The dark figure had left them alone for now, but they couldn't afford to wait too long.

When they arrived, Victor quickly explained the plan. "Listen, we've got a chance to get the book. There's a gathering, and Noxmire will be addressing everyone. It'll be the perfect distraction."

Clara's eyes widened. "A gathering? So everyone will be in one place? That's... perfect!"

Brumble grinned, always eager for action. "I'll make sure the book is ours by the time Noxmire is done. You can count on me."

Victor gave them both a serious look. "We don't have much time. You need to get to the book when everyone's distracted. Once you have it, we'll get the crystal from Noxmire's back. We can trap him once and for all."

Clara nodded, her resolve strengthening. "We'll do our part. You and Gruffle stay in position and make sure Noxmire stays distracted. We'll handle the book."

Victor and Gruffle turned to leave, heading toward the gathering. They had to stay hidden and make sure they didn't draw any attention. As they moved through the halls of the palace, Victor's thoughts were already racing ahead to what they had to do next. Time was ticking away, and every second counted.

The gathering was being held in a grand, dark hall at the heart of Noxmire's palace. The hall was filled with dark figures, all of Noxmire's most loyal followers. They were seated in rows, their eyes gleaming with an unsettling hunger. The air was thick with the scent of fear and anticipation.

When Victor and Gruffle arrived, they blended in with the other guards, trying their best not to attract attention. They found a quiet corner near the front of the hall, where Noxmire would soon stand to speak.

Noxmire's voice suddenly rang out, commanding the attention of everyone in the room. "My loyal subjects," he said, his voice cold and powerful. "Tonight, we take the next step toward total domination. The world of Drakoria is ours for the taking, and soon, no one will be able to stop us."

The crowd murmured with excitement, their dark eyes glinting with malice. Noxmire's speech went on, outlining his plans to expand his dark rule and crush any remaining resistance. But while he spoke, Victor's mind was elsewhere. He could already hear Brumble and Clara making their move.

Meanwhile, back in the chamber where the Holy Drake Book rested, Brumble and Clara were ready. They stood still, watching the door as the minutes ticked by. Clara's heart was racing, but Brumble remained calm as ever.

"We need to wait for the perfect moment," Clara whispered. "Once Noxmire is fully distracted, we make our move."

Brumble's eyes sparkled with mischief. "You know what they say—fortune favors the bold."

Clara shot him a small smile, but it was quickly replaced by a look of focus. "Okay, now!"

They both moved swiftly and silently toward the pedestal, keeping their heads down to avoid being seen. The chamber was quiet, save for the faint sounds of Noxmire's speech echoing through the hall. With every step, Clara's heart seemed to beat louder in her chest, but she pushed the fear aside.

Brumble reached out, carefully lifting the Holy Drake Book from its pedestal. As his fingers brushed against it, a faint glow filled the room, but he quickly shut it down with a soft hiss.

"We have to be quick," Clara urged, her voice barely above a whisper.

Brumble nodded, keeping the book hidden under his arm as they backed away from the pedestal. "Let's go. We don't have long."

As they made their way out of the chamber, Clara's mind raced with what they had to do next. The crystal from Noxmire's back was the final key. Once they had that, they could trap him and close the portals to all worlds.

Outside the chamber, they joined Victor and Gruffle, who were still keeping an eye on the gathering. The moment Noxmire finished his speech, the guards would be distracted, giving them just enough time to get close and take the crystal.

Victor was watching Noxmire, who was now finishing up his speech. The dark lord's power was palpable, filling the hall with an energy that made it hard to breathe. But this was it—their one chance to take the final step.

As Noxmire raised his arms to signal the end of his speech, the crowd erupted into applause. Victor and Gruffle quickly moved to the front, staying in the shadows. They didn't want to get too close just yet. The time wasn't right.

The applause slowly died down, and Noxmire turned to leave the stage, his guards following behind him. This was the moment.

Victor and Gruffle pushed forward, their footsteps quick and determined. They needed to get to Noxmire before anyone noticed them.

Back in the chamber with the Holy Drake Book, Brumble and Clara waited. They knew that the next phase of their plan had to go off without a hitch. They had the book. Now, they needed to find a way to retrieve the crystal from Noxmire's back, the final step in their mission.

"We're almost there," Clara said quietly, glancing at Brumble. "We just have to be patient."

Brumble nodded, his eyes darting between the shadows and the hallway leading to the gathering. "Don't worry. We've got this."

The tension in the palace was palpable as Victor, Gruffle, Brumble, and Clara all moved into position. The gathering was still underway, but their time was running out. Noxmire was distracted, and this was their golden opportunity to finish what they had started.

The tension in the air was thick, like a storm waiting to break. Noxmire had gathered all the new recruits, lining them up in rows as he inspected each one carefully. His dark eyes swept over them, scanning for any sign of suspicion. Victor and Gruffle, both pretending to be just another set of guards, stood among the recruits, doing their best to blend in with the crowd.

Victor's heart raced in his chest. He could feel the eyes of Noxmire on him, and he knew that the dark lord would sense something was off the moment he got too close. His palms were sweaty, and his mind raced with plans to escape if things went wrong. But there was no turning back now.

Noxmire's voice echoed through the chamber, a cold, commanding tone. "Welcome, new recruits," he said. "You've been chosen to serve under my command. You will be tested. And those who are worthy will rise to the top. But those who are not... will be trapped. You will become part of my eternal army."

The recruits stiffened, their eyes wide with fear. Victor swallowed hard. He had to keep his composure. His turn was fast approaching, and when it came, he knew he had to act quickly.

As Victor stepped forward, Noxmire's eyes narrowed. He could tell there was something about this new recruit that didn't sit right with him. Victor tried to hide his nervousness, but the dark lord wasn't fooled.

"You," Noxmire said, his voice dripping with suspicion. "You are different. What is your name?"

Victor's throat tightened. "Victor," he said, trying to sound confident.

Noxmire stepped closer, his eyes scanning Victor's face with an unnerving intensity. "Victor," he repeated. "A simple name for someone who is hiding something."

Victor's heart pounded. He could feel the trap closing around him. Just as Noxmire raised his hand to use his dark powers to trap Victor in a cage of shadows, something unexpected happened.

In an instant, Victor reached out and snatched the crystal from the back of Noxmire's cloak. The moment his fingers touched it, a surge of power shot through his body. Noxmire's eyes widened in shock, and he let out an agonizing scream. The entire palace seemed to tremble, the walls groaning as though the very foundation of the world was shaking.

"NOOO!" Noxmire howled in fury. His dark magic swirled around him, but it was too late. The crystal had been removed, and his control over the palace was slipping away.

All around them, the guards turned with enraged expressions, their eyes glowing with dark energy. They were ready to strike, but before they could move, Brumble and Clara burst into the room, running with incredible speed. Their eyes were filled with determination, and they didn't hesitate for a moment. They knew exactly what they had to do.

As the guards charged toward them, Gruffle stood his ground, brandishing his weapons to defend the group. He shouted to Brumble and Clara, "Get to the book! I'll hold them off!"

Victor, still holding the crystal, saw Clara leap toward him in one smooth motion, her hands outstretched. "Throw it!" she yelled, her voice full of urgency.

Without thinking twice, Victor hurled the crystal toward Clara. She jumped from a nearby table, her body twisting gracefully through the air, and snatched the crystal from the air in a perfect, heroic catch.

Clara's heart raced as she landed on the ground, the crystal now firmly in her grasp. Without wasting a second, she sprinted to the Holy Drake Book, which Brumble had already grabbed. The atmosphere in the palace seemed to darken, the air thick with the energy of the trapped spirits trying to escape. Clara didn't hesitate. She placed the crystal into the book.

The moment the crystal touched the pages, the entire room seemed to go cold. The temperature dropped, and an unnatural darkness flooded the chamber. The ground trembled, and fireballs began to rain down from the ceiling, lighting up the room like a hellish storm.

Brumble, Clara, Victor, and Gruffle all felt the pressure building as the atmosphere grew heavier. Brumble quickly opened the book, the powerful magic swirling around him. The book emitted a blinding light, and they all gritted their teeth as the energy surged.

"We have to hold it open!" Brumble shouted, his voice strained. "If it closes, everything we've done will be for nothing!"

Victor, Clara, and Gruffle rushed to Brumble's side, each of them using all their strength to help keep the book open.

The power pouring from the book was almost too much to handle, like a storm of pure magic. They screamed in pain as the book fought against them, the weight of the evil spirits trapped within it pulling at their very souls.

Noxmire, now furious beyond reason, tried to reach for the book, his hands shaking with rage. "You cannot trap me!" he shouted. "You cannot contain me!"

But it was too late. The evil spirits, including Noxmire himself, were being sucked into the pages of the Holy Drake Book. The palace shook as the spirits wailed, their voices echoing through the hall. It felt like the very fabric of reality was tearing apart as the book absorbed their power.

Clara, Brumble, and Victor screamed, holding the book open with all their might. The pain was unbearable, but they couldn't stop. They had to finish what they had started.

Finally, with one last scream of defiance from Noxmire, the book slammed shut with a deafening thud. The dark energy in the room instantly vanished, leaving only silence behind.

The palace was still.

Victor, Clara, Brumble, and Gruffle collapsed to the ground, exhausted and battered from the immense strain. They had done it. Noxmire was trapped, his evil spirit sealed within the pages of the Holy Drake Book.

For a long moment, no one spoke. The only sound was the heavy breathing of the group, as they tried to recover from the ordeal.

Finally, Victor looked up, a faint smile on his face. "We did it," he said, his voice hoarse but filled with triumph.

Brumble grinned, wiping sweat from his brow. "Yeah. We really did."

Clara sat up slowly, her expression a mixture of exhaustion and relief. "Drakoria is safe. We stopped him."

Gruffle chuckled, brushing off his clothes. "Not bad for a group of newbies."

Together, they stood in the dark, quiet palace, knowing that their battle was won, but their journey was far from over. They had saved Drakoria from Noxmire's evil, but now they had to figure out how to restore balance to the world and protect it from any new threats that might arise.

For now, though, they allowed themselves a moment of peace. Their mission was complete. The Holy Drake Book had done its job, and the evil that had threatened their world was finally sealed away for good.

And so, with the crystal still glowing faintly in Clara's hand and the book secured, they left the dark palace behind.

As the final echoes of the evil spirits trapped within the Holy Drake Book faded into nothingness, the atmosphere around the group began to shift. The darkness that had consumed the air of Noxmire's palace—the heavy, oppressive weight that had crushed every breath they took—slowly lifted. The jagged, red sky that had loomed above them like an endless storm cloud began to change, lightening into something far more serene and beautiful.

The sky turned a deep, rich shade of blue, as if a new dawn had come. The air itself seemed to feel lighter, purer. The ground beneath their feet, once cold and unforgiving, now felt warm, soft—like the earth had been reborn.

Victor, Clara, Brumble, and Gruffle all stood there, breathless, as the scene before them unfolded. For a long moment, none of them moved. Their eyes were wide in awe, as if they were witnessing a miracle unfold before them.

The plants that had been wilting in the harsh, dark atmosphere of the palace began to stir, their leaves trembling as they opened up. Buds on flowers bloomed before their eyes, bursting into vibrant, brilliant colors that painted the air with their beauty. A soft, melodic hum seemed to rise from the earth itself, as if the land was singing in harmony with the new, pure energy that had flooded the world.

In the distance, the moon still hung high in the sky, but it was no longer alone. Two other suns, golden and radiant, began to rise, breaking through the darkened clouds that had remained even after Noxmire's defeat. The two suns, though unfamiliar, were warm and comforting, their light soft and inviting. As they came closer together, their radiance merged in the sky, casting beams of light that shimmered in every color imaginable. It was as if the universe itself was painting the world with new hope.

The two suns moved closer to one another until they almost touched, their light creating a strange, ethereal bridge of energy that arced through the sky. This glowing passage seemed to hum with an otherworldly vibrancy. It was as if the very air was alive, pulsing with the souls of the long-lost spirits, now free from the clutches of darkness.

Victor's eyes filled with wonder as he took in the scene. "What is this?" he whispered in awe.

"It's... it's like a new world is being born," Clara said, her voice trembling with a mix of excitement and disbelief. "The land, the sky... it's all changing."

Brumble stood beside them, his eyes sparkling with the realization of their victory. "We did it. We really did it. We freed Drakoria from Noxmire's curse."

Gruffle let out a deep breath, his shoulders relaxing for the first time in what felt like ages. "I can't believe it. This place—it feels... peaceful. Like something beautiful is being reborn."

The air around them shimmered, and they could feel the wind begin to stir, but it wasn't the harsh, cold wind they had encountered before. This breeze was warm, gentle, filled with the fragrance of new life. It passed through their hair, across their skin, as if it were carrying the essence of all the good that had been awakened in Drakoria. It was as though the earth was breathing again.

Suddenly, the vibrant, colorful wind began to swirl around them, weaving through the air in ribbons of light. It was as if the souls that had been trapped—those who had fought for Drakoria and the light—were now free, dancing with joy and leaving traces of their energy behind. The colors of the wind seemed to speak to each of them, offering a quiet, comforting reassurance that everything they had done had been worth it.

Victor felt the warmth of the light wash over him, and his heart swelled with a deep sense of peace. "It's... it's like the world is healing," he murmured. "Like all the suffering is fading away."

Clara nodded, her voice filled with emotion. "We've done something incredible. Noxmire is gone. The darkness is over. Drakoria is free."

Brumble clenched his fists, a smile tugging at his lips. "And we were a part of it. We saved the world."

Gruffle's gruff demeanor softened as he gazed at the transforming landscape, his eyes reflecting the colors of the wind. "I didn't think it would feel like this. I thought it would be... darker. But this? This is beautiful. It's like a whole new beginning."

The swirling wind began to settle, and the vibrant light that filled the air slowly faded, leaving behind a landscape of breathtaking beauty. The sun's rays grew warmer, casting golden beams across the now lush landscape. The trees were no longer twisted and dark; they were tall and strong, their leaves rich with life. Flowers bloomed in every color imaginable, covering the ground in a blanket of softness. The river that ran through the palace grounds sparkled as though it had been purified by the very energy of the sun.

For the first time in what felt like forever, the group stood in a world full of hope and possibility. The land that had been ravaged by darkness and despair now shimmered with a vibrant new life, its potential endless.

Victor turned to his friends, his eyes bright with joy and determination. "This is just the beginning. We've defeated Noxmire, but there's so much more to do. Drakoria can rebuild itself, but we have to help it. Together."

Clara smiled, her face lighting up with the same sense of hope. "Yes. This world needs us. And we'll be here to protect it."

Brumble gave a loud cheer, leaping into the air. "Drakoria is free! We did it!"

Gruffle looked out across the newly reborn land, the sun's light glinting off his armor. He took a deep breath, his voice steady and proud. "This place will be ours to protect. But for now... we rest. We've earned it."

As the group stood there, the two suns in the sky slowly began to rise higher, casting their golden light over Drakoria. The once-ruined land was now a place of life, rebirth, and endless possibility. A world where the forces of darkness had been defeated, and the light had reclaimed its rightful place.

For Victor, Clara, Brumble, and Gruffle, their journey was far from over. But for the first time in a long while, they felt the weight of their mission lift, replaced by the promise of hope, the power of the world's renewal, and the strength they had found within each other.

Drakoria had been saved. And now, with the land healing, their adventure was only just beginning.

As soon as the evil spirits were trapped inside the Holy Drake Book and it was finally closed, everything changed. The black sky that had loomed over the land for so long turned bright blue, and the air smelled fresh and clean. Flowers that had been dead for centuries suddenly began to bloom, their colors bright and happy. The dark and gloomy world that had been controlled by Noxmire was now a peaceful, beautiful place.

But that wasn't all. The two new suns that had appeared in the sky began to shine even brighter. They started to get closer to each other, as if they were dancing in the sky. Their light made the air look colorful, almost like rainbows swirling all around. The colors felt warm and full of life, as if the very land itself was coming alive again, filling the air with happiness.

Then, something magical happened. The swirling colors began to take shape. The souls of the ancient spirits, who had been trapped for so long, started to form into creatures. These creatures were kind and gentle, and they seemed to be made of light and color, the same light that had been released from the book. The creatures walked around, looking at the world in wonder, and they helped the land become even more beautiful.

As the creatures continued to form, a bright light appeared in front of the group. It was so powerful that it made everyone stop in their tracks. The light began to fade, revealing three incredible figures standing before them. Victor, Clara, Brumble, and Gruffle gasped in surprise. They could hardly believe their eyes. Standing before them were King Drake, Queen Dracia, and Milo-Blaze, the mighty dragon who had helped them so much on their journey.

It was them. King Drake, the ruler of Drakoria, and his beautiful wife, Queen Dracia, had returned. Milo-Blaze, the powerful dragon, stood beside them, his fiery scales glowing warmly. The group of friends knelt down in awe, unable to speak at first. They had heard the stories of these great leaders, but they had never imagined they would actually meet them.

King Drake was the first to speak. His voice was deep and warm, like the sound of thunder in the distance. "Brave ones," he said, "you have done something incredible. You have freed our world from the darkness. We have watched from afar, waiting for someone strong enough to defeat Noxmire. And now, we stand before you, proud of what you have accomplished."

Tears filled Victor's eyes as he looked up at the king. He had never felt so honored in his life. "We did it together," he said, his voice shaking. "We couldn't have done it without you. You gave us the strength to keep going."

Queen Dracia smiled gently. Her silver wings shimmered as she spoke. "You are the true heroes of Drakoria," she said softly. "You are the ones who saved our land. Your courage has brought light back to Drakoria, and for that, we are forever grateful."

Milo-Blaze nodded proudly. "The land is free now. The darkness is gone. You have done what no one thought possible. You are the new protectors of Drakoria."

Clara, feeling overwhelmed by everything that had happened, stepped forward. "We couldn't have done it without your guidance," she said, wiping away tears. "We were just trying to help, but you showed us how to believe in ourselves."

Brumble, his usual boisterous self, was speechless. He looked at King Drake, Queen Dracia, and Milo-Blaze, unable to find the right words. Instead, he bowed deeply, his eyes filled with respect and admiration.

Victor turned to his friends, his heart swelling with pride. "We did it," he said, his voice full of joy. "We saved Drakoria. And now, we're going to protect it, together."

King Drake smiled, his golden scales gleaming. "Yes, you will protect it. Drakoria is yours now, and it will always be your home. You are the guardians of this land, the ones who will make sure it stays safe and full of light."

The group stood tall, ready for whatever came next. They had faced great challenges, but they had proven themselves worthy. They had saved Drakoria, and now, they would ensure that the world stayed safe, protected, and full of life.

As they stood together, the two suns in the sky grew even brighter, casting their warm, golden light over the land. The wind blew gently, carrying the sound of laughter and joy through the air. The creatures that had been born from the souls of the spirits danced and played, filling the world with happiness.

Victor, Clara, Brumble, and Gruffle stood tall, their hearts full of hope and determination. They knew that their journey was far from over. They had just begun their new role as protectors of Drakoria, but they were ready. They would face whatever challenges came their way, together.

And as they looked up at the sky, the light of the two suns shining down on them, they knew one thing for sure: the world was finally at peace, and it was their job to keep it that way.

With King Drake, Queen Dracia, and Milo-Blaze by their side, they would keep Drakoria safe, forever.

Everyone stood in awe, still feeling the weight of their victory. The sun's warm light bathed the land, and the creatures of Drakoria danced around, celebrating their newfound freedom. It felt like the world had been reborn. Victor couldn't help but feel a strange sensation, as though a deep connection was pulling at his heart. He closed his eyes for a moment, letting the joy of the moment wash over him.

Then, in the stillness, a faint voice reached his ears. It was soft, but filled with warmth, like the sound of wind through the trees. "Victor," the voice called.

Victor's eyes snapped open, and he looked around in surprise. His heart skipped a beat as the voice grew clearer. It was a voice he hadn't heard in so long—his grandpa's voice.

"Grandpa?" Victor whispered, a mix of disbelief and hope in his voice.

The voice answered, and though it wasn't physical, it was clear in his heart. "I'm so proud of you, Victor. You've done what I couldn't. You've freed the land and saved Drakoria. I've been watching over you, and now, my soul is free."

Victor's eyes filled with tears, his heart overflowing with emotion. He could feel his grandpa's presence—his love, his pride—and for the first time in a long while, he felt the weight of loss lift from his chest. It was like the final piece of the puzzle had clicked into place. His grandpa's spirit was at peace.

"I did it... I finally did it," Victor whispered, looking up at the sky as if his grandpa were watching him from the heavens.

The moment was interrupted when King Drake, his warm golden scales shimmering in the light, stepped forward. "Victor," he said, his voice gentle but serious. "There is still one more task to complete. The world is not fully restored yet."

Everyone turned to him, confused. They had freed Drakoria, trapped Noxmire's spirit, and watched the sky change from black to blue. What else could there be?

Drake nodded, as if he had anticipated their confusion. "We are not completely here yet. What you see before you is just our souls, trapped between worlds. To fully restore everything and bring us back completely, you must destroy the Obsidian Compass."

The words hung in the air, heavy with meaning. The group exchanged glances, trying to understand.

"The Obsidian Compass?" Clara asked, her brow furrowed. "What is it? Where is it?"

"It is an ancient artifact that Noxmire used to maintain his control over the portals," Drake explained. "It is a powerful object that has the ability to lock away all the portals connected to different worlds. Without it, the portals cannot stay open, and the spirits of Drakoria will be free to return completely. But only by destroying the compass can we break the final ties that bind us to this world. It is the key to returning to full form."

Victor's heart raced as he thought about the task ahead. "Where is the Obsidian Compass? How do we find it?"

Drake lifted his head, and his gaze seemed to look far into the distance. "The Holy Drake Book will guide you. You must follow the path that it lays out for you. The compass is hidden in a place beyond this land, a place where the last remnants of Noxmire's power still linger."

Brumble, always eager for adventure, stepped forward. "We'll do it! We'll find it and destroy it, no matter where it is."

Milo-Blaze, who had been standing quietly beside King Drake, nodded in agreement. "The task is not easy, but you have already proven your strength and courage. Trust in the book, and it will show you the way."

Victor looked at his friends—Clara, Brumble, Gruffle—and then at King Drake. He could feel the weight of the responsibility ahead, but he also felt a fire inside him, a desire to finish what they had started. They had come this far, and there was no turning back.

"Then let's go," Victor said, his voice filled with determination. "We'll destroy the Obsidian Compass, and we'll bring Drakoria back to life. We'll make sure everything is truly free."

The group gathered around King Drake, who smiled at them with pride. "You are true heroes. And once you destroy the compass, our world will be fully restored. The skies will be clear, the lands will be peaceful, and the spirits will return to their rightful places."

With the Holy Drake Book in hand and their hearts full of purpose, the group set off once more. They had already overcome so much, and now they faced their final task. As they walked away from the vibrant, newly restored Drakoria, the two suns in the sky seemed to shine even brighter, as if to guide their way.

The book's pages glowed softly, its magic still guiding them forward, showing them the way to the final battle.

Victor, Clara, Brumble, Gruffle, and Milo-Blaze, all guided by the Holy Drake Book, traveled through the restored land of Drakoria. Their journey led them to a mysterious, mist-covered valley, unlike anything they had encountered before. The valley seemed to pulse with an eerie energy, and the air grew thick, making it hard to breathe. The path ahead was uncertain, but the book continued to glow, pointing the way to the location of the Obsidian Compass.

"This place feels... wrong," Clara said, her voice filled with unease. "It's as if the land itself is holding its breath."

Victor glanced at her and nodded. "I feel it too. The further we go, the more it feels like we're being watched."

Brumble, ever the optimist, tried to cheer everyone up. "Come on, guys! We've faced worse! We've got this!" he said, though his usual confidence was tinged with uncertainty.

Milo-Blaze's massive wings stirred the mist as he soared above them, scanning the area. "Stay alert," the dragon warned. "This valley is not a friendly place. Noxmire's influence still lingers here. We must be cautious."

The Holy Drake Book began to glow even brighter as they walked deeper into the valley. The path was narrow, winding, and covered in thick vines. The mist grew heavier, and the once-clear sky above seemed to darken. As they ventured forward, the atmosphere seemed to press down on them, as if the world itself was trying to stop them.

"Look out!" Brumble suddenly shouted, pointing ahead. A thick wall of brambles rose from the ground, blocking their way. The vines twisted and writhed as if alive, snaking toward them with sharp, thorny tendrils.

Clara took a step back, her heart racing. "How do we get past that?"

Victor stepped forward, gripping the Holy Drake Book tightly. The pages fluttered as if guided by an unseen hand. He quickly flipped through the pages, looking for answers. "We have to pass the challenge of the Thorns," he read aloud. "The path will test our strength and our resolve. Only those with pure hearts can pass."

"This is no time for riddles," Brumble grumbled. "Let's just break through!"

Before anyone could argue, Milo-Blaze landed in front of the brambles, his massive claws sinking into the earth. "Wait," he said calmly. "We will not break through with force alone. Let me try something."

The dragon closed his eyes, his body glowing faintly. He lifted his head toward the sky, as if drawing strength from the very air around him. Slowly, the brambles began to slow their movement, the tendrils pulling back ever so slightly.

"I can calm the vines," Milo-Blaze said. "But we must move quickly. The longer we stay, the more dangerous this place becomes."

Victor nodded. "We'll move as one. Stay close."

With the dragon leading the way, they moved carefully through the mist, the brambles retreating just enough to allow them passage. As they ventured deeper into the valley, the land seemed to grow more ominous, the mist thickening and the sky dimming further. But they pressed on, knowing they were close to their goal.

The path soon narrowed, and they came upon a large stone door embedded in the side of a mountain. The Holy Drake Book's pages began to glow brightly, pointing directly to the door. It was as if the book had been leading them here all along.

"This must be it," Victor said, looking at the door with awe. "The Obsidian Compass is behind this door."

Milo-Blaze stepped forward, his fiery gaze scanning the door. "It's not going to be that easy," he warned. "There will be another challenge, one that tests our unity."

As if on cue, the ground beneath their feet began to rumble. The stone door started to glow, and strange, ancient symbols appeared on its surface. Suddenly, the symbols began to pulse, and a voice echoed from the stone, deep and foreboding.

"To enter, you must prove that your hearts are united," the voice boomed. "Each of you must face a trial alone. Only by overcoming your greatest fears will the door open."

Victor felt his stomach twist with dread. A trial? Alone? He wasn't sure if he was ready for that. But there was no turning back now.

The voice continued, "Each fear will be unique. Face it with courage, or remain forever trapped in this place."

Clara stepped forward first, her face set with determination. "I'll go first," she said, her voice steady, though her hands trembled. She had faced many challenges, but this was different. Her fear was deep and personal.

As she stepped toward the door, the world around her changed. The mist vanished, and she found herself in a dark forest. The trees were twisted and gnarled, and the ground beneath her feet felt cold. In the distance, she saw a figure—her mother, who had disappeared long ago, standing alone in the forest.

"Mom?" Clara called out, her voice cracking with emotion.

The figure turned, and Clara's heart raced. But as the figure came closer, it changed. It became a shadow, a dark reflection of her mother's face, filled with pain and anger. Clara could feel her fear rising, but she forced herself to stay calm.

"Don't fear," Clara whispered to herself. "This isn't real."

The shadow lunged at her, but Clara stood her ground. She closed her eyes and reached deep within herself, drawing on the strength she had found during her journey. Slowly, the shadow faded, and the forest around her brightened. The fear was gone. Clara had faced her fear of losing loved ones, and she had conquered it.

The door rumbled, and a small section of it began to open. Clara stepped back, breathing heavily, but with a sense of victory. She had done it.

Next was Brumble. He strode forward confidently, ready to face whatever lay ahead. The door shimmered, and the mist swirled around him, forming into a shadowy version of himself. It was a dark, twisted version, taller and more menacing. The shadow growled at him, its voice mocking.

"You're nothing," it hissed. "You'll never be good enough."

Brumble clenched his fists, anger bubbling inside him. The shadow sneered, its grin wide and malicious.

"You've always been a fool," the shadow taunted. "No one respects you. No one believes in you."

But Brumble stood tall. He was no longer the uncertain, insecure boy who had doubted himself. He had proven his worth countless times on this journey. With a roar, he charged at the shadow, his voice steady and strong. "I am who I am, and that's enough!"

The shadow screamed as it vanished, and the mist cleared. The door rumbled again, and another section of it opened.

Gruffle was next. He stepped forward, his usual confidence shaken by the challenge. The mist parted, and in its place stood a vast, dark pit. The ground around it cracked and crumbled, and from the depths of the pit, a shadowy figure rose—his father, the one who had always told him he would never amount to anything.

"You'll fall," the figure hissed. "You'll always be a failure. You're nothing like me."

Gruffle's heart pounded, but he didn't back down. "I'm not like you," he said firmly. "And that's a good thing."

With a fierce cry, Gruffle leaped into the pit, and as he did, the shadowy figure dissolved into mist. Gruffle had faced his fear of not being good enough, and he had proven it wrong.

Finally, it was Victor's turn. He stepped forward, his mind racing with doubt. As the door opened, the mist swirled around him, and he was transported to a dark, quiet place—a place that felt cold and empty. In front of him stood a figure, familiar and yet distant. It was his grandpa, the one who had always been his guide and protector.

"I knew you'd fail," the figure said in a cold, mocking tone. "You never could save Drakoria. You were never good enough to carry on the family legacy."

Victor's heart shattered at the words. His grandpa had always been his hero, and the thought of not living up to that legacy filled him with fear and guilt. But then, he remembered everything he had been through—the strength he had gained, the lessons he had learned, and the friends who had stood by him. He wasn't alone anymore.

"No," Victor said firmly, his voice steady. "I am strong. I am enough. I will carry the legacy, and I will save Drakoria."

The figure dissolved into mist, and the door groaned as it finally opened fully. They had passed the trial.

The group walked through the door, their hearts filled with determination. They had faced their deepest fears and come out victorious. Ahead of them stood the Obsidian Compass, its dark power radiating through the room. The final task was within their reach.

17

As the group stood before the Obsidian Compass, the weight of the moment settled on their shoulders like an unshakeable burden. The air around them hummed with dark energy, and the compass pulsed with a sinister, magnetic force. It was clear that this was the final step to seal Noxmire's influence once and for all.

Milo-Blaze, his fiery eyes filled with the gravity of the situation, spoke solemnly. "This compass must be destroyed, but be warned. Once you do, the portals to all worlds, including Earth, will close forever. There will be no going back. You will be trapped here, in Drakoria, for good."

The group fell silent, the enormity of his words sinking in. They had all come so far, facing unimaginable trials, battling dark forces, and now they were at the precipice of their final victory. Yet the cost was heavy—no more Earth, no more home. The thought of never seeing their world again, of never being able to return, was a thought that none of them had truly allowed themselves to fully consider.

Milo-Blaze continued, his voice soft but resolute. "Only one of you can destroy the compass. Either Clara or Victor. It is a decision you must make together. The reason for this is simple: the dark magic that has tainted you, being in Noxmire's territory for so long, must be erased by someone who has not been as deeply affected. Only one of you can sever the connection to the darkness."

Clara and Victor exchanged a long, lingering look. It was hard to imagine a world without each other, but Milo-Blaze's words rang true. One of them had to destroy the compass, or the evil would persist, lingering in the air like a faint shadow, ready to rise again.

Milo-Blaze took a deep breath, activating the compass with a magical pulse. A swirling portal to Earth opened in front of them, glowing brightly with the light of their home world. The sight of the portal brought a sense of longing to their hearts. It was like seeing a distant memory, a dream that was slowly slipping away.

Victor's heart ached as he looked at Clara. She was standing next to him, her eyes wide with uncertainty and fear. He knew what had to be done, but he couldn't help feeling a deep sadness welling up inside him. If he stayed behind, he would be trapped in Drakoria forever, never able to return to his family, his friends, or his home. But he couldn't risk the chance of failure, the chance of the darkness finding a way to return.

With a heavy heart, Victor turned to Clara, his voice trembling. "Clara, you have to go. I'll stay here and destroy the compass. You've been through so much, and you deserve to go home. I can't let the darkness follow us back. I can't let Earth suffer because of me."

Clara's eyes filled with tears as she shook her head, her voice breaking. "No, Victor. I can't leave you here. We've been through everything together. We're a team. I'm not going to leave you behind." Her hands trembled as she reached for his, her touch warm but desperate. "You've always been there for me, for all of us. We promised we'd finish this together."

Victor held her hand tightly, his own tears threatening to spill. "I know, but sometimes, you have to make the hard choices. And this is one of them. Drakoria needs us both. If we're both in the same place when the compass is destroyed, we risk everything. The darkness might still find a way to break free. I can't let that happen."

Clara's heart shattered as she looked into his eyes. The thought of leaving him behind, of facing this final challenge without him, was unbearable. But Victor was right. The world they had fought for, the world they loved, depended on this choice. If they were both tied to the same place when the compass was destroyed, they would be giving Noxmire the chance to rise again. They couldn't allow that to happen.

"I don't want to leave you," Clara whispered, tears falling freely now. "But... I understand. You're right. You have to stay here, Victor. But promise me, promise me we'll find a way back to each other. Promise me that we'll be reunited."

Victor squeezed her hand, his voice steady despite the storm of emotions inside him. "I promise. No matter what happens, Clara, I'll find a way back to you. We've made it this far. I know we can make it through anything."

The moment stretched on, each of them holding onto the other, unwilling to let go, but knowing it was the only way to ensure that Drakoria, and all the worlds connected to it, would be safe. Their souls were intertwined by the bond they had shared on this journey, and that bond would not fade, no matter how far apart they would be.

With a final, lingering kiss on her forehead, Victor slowly stepped away from Clara, his heart breaking with every step. The portal to Earth still hovered before them, the bright light calling to them, but it was not for them anymore. Not for Victor. Not for Clara.

Milo-Blaze spoke softly, his voice filled with understanding. "The time has come, Victor, Clara. You have both shown immense strength. Now, you must both show the courage to face the end, knowing that it is only the beginning of a new chapter."

Victor nodded, his gaze never leaving Clara. "Go, Clara. Go and live the life you deserve."

Clara hesitated for a moment longer before stepping toward the portal, her heart heavy with sorrow, but filled with the same fierce determination that had carried her through every trial. She looked back one last time, her eyes meeting Victor's.

"I love you, Victor," she said softly, her voice filled with a strength he knew came from deep within her.

"I love you too, Clara," he whispered back, his voice barely audible over the beating of his own heart. "Now go. For both of us."

With a final glance, Clara stepped through the portal, leaving Victor behind. As the portal closed behind her, Victor felt an emptiness settle in his chest. The world beyond had just become a little bit smaller, and his path had become a little more uncertain. But he had made the right choice.

Victor turned back to the Obsidian Compass, his hands shaking as he prepared to destroy it. The compass had been the source of all the darkness, all the pain, all the trials. But now, it was time to put an end to it, to ensure that no one else would suffer from Noxmire's curse ever again.

He raised his hand and slammed it down onto the compass, the force of the blow sending a shockwave through the air. The compass cracked, and an explosion of light filled the room, blinding Victor momentarily. When the light faded, he looked down and saw that the compass was gone—destroyed.

The ground beneath him shook, and for a moment, he feared the worst. But as the tremors died down, he felt the world around him shift. The air was lighter, the oppressive weight of darkness lifting. He had done it. He had destroyed the Obsidian Compass, sealed Noxmire's power forever, and closed the portals to all worlds.

Victor dropped to his knees, exhausted and overwhelmed by the enormity of what had just happened. He had saved the worlds, but at such a heavy price. His heart ached for Clara, for the friends he had left behind, and for the world that would now carry on without him.

But despite the pain, Victor knew he had made the right choice. Drakoria was safe. And that was all that mattered.

And as he looked toward the horizon, where the two suns now blazed in the sky, he knew that somehow, someday, their story would continue. The love and bond he shared with Clara would transcend the boundaries of this world.

As the souls of King Drake, Queen Dracia, Milo-Blaze, and all the other brave souls of Drakoria fully appeared, the entire land was filled with joy. Hundreds, even thousands of Drakorians, cheered and chanted, "Victor! Victor!" Their voices echoed through the skies, celebrating Victor as the hero who had saved their world.

Victor stood there, overwhelmed with happiness, as everyone surrounded him, thanking him, praising him, and calling him the savior of Drakoria. King Drake and Queen Dracia hugged him tightly, proud of his bravery and sacrifice. Milo-Blaze roared with pride, and the entire kingdom rejoiced.

But even with all the joy around him, Victor's heart felt a little heavy. He looked around, searching for Clara. He missed her. He wished she could have been there to share this moment with him.

He knew Drakoria was safe, but he couldn't help feeling like a piece of his heart was still with her. Still, he smiled, knowing that his journey wasn't over. He had saved Drakoria, and now he would protect it forever.

The End

Clara returned to Earth, heartbroken but resolute. She dedicated her life to protecting the fragile balance between worlds, ensuring no one would repeat Victor's mistake. As for Victor, legends in Drakoria spoke of a man who walked among dragons, a mortal who defied the Dragonlords and safeguarded the realm from destruction.

Though separated by worlds, Clara never lost hope. Every night, she gazed at the stars, whispering a silent prayer to the man she loved, believing that one day, their paths would cross again.

Nishi Shah, Age-15

Nishi Shah is the author of Drakoria, her debut novel. With a strong passion for storytelling, she creates exciting and imaginative worlds filled with magic, adventure, and memorable characters. Drakoria is the first step in her journey as a writer, blending her love for myths, fantasy, and storytelling to offer readers an enjoyable escape.

Nishi is inspired by the rich history of myths and legends from different cultures, which shape her writing. She focuses on themes like bravery, friendship, and personal growth, hoping to inspire readers through her stories.

As she continues her writing journey, Drakoria is just the beginning of the many stories she plans to share with readers. Happy Reading!

www.ingramcontent.com/pod-product-compliance
Lightning Source LLC
Chambersburg PA
CBHW031038160726
47991CB00005B/1940